Table of Co[ntents]

Hollywood Quotes 3
1 – Hollywood 4
2 – Tip-Off 7
3 – Red Roses 11
4 – Anonymous 18
5 – Beverly Hills Hotel 23
6 – The Mistress 29
7 – Stone 36
8 – Best Friends 45
9 – Perino's 52
10 – Opportunities 59
11 – 'A Pocketful of Coins' 65
12 – Willoughby 70
13 – Arthur 77
14 – New Beginning 83
15 – Garden Party 89
16 – Bella & Boris 95
17 – Mind Games 102
18 – Hollenbeck Park 110
19 – The Observatory 116
20 – Two-Toned Wingtips 122
21 – Bullock's 128
22 – Ruth 134
23 – Missing 139
24 – The Photograph 146
25 – Sunset Strip 152
26 – Payback 159
27 – A Daring Move 164
28 – Until We Meet Again 171
A Special Note to Readers 176

A PERILOUS PREMIERE

STONE & STEELE
Book One

GAIL MEATH

Stone & Steele Mysteries 1930s:

A Perilous Premiere, Book One
A Bloody Banquet, Book Two (2025)

Jax Diamond Mysteries 1920s:

Songbird, Book 1
Framed, Book 2
Deuce, Book 3
Two of a Kind, Book 4
Blackjack, Book 5
Killjoy, Book 6
The Diamonds, Book 7
Wildcard, Book 8 (April 2025)
Cranberry Pond Publishing
www.gailmeath.com[1]

Copyright © 2024 by Gail Meath

All rights reserved. This book or any portion thereof may not be reproduced or used in any manner without the express written permission of the publisher, except for the use of brief quotations in a book review. This book is a work of fiction. Names, characters, places, and incidents are the product of the author's imagination or are used fictitiously. Any resemblance to actual events, locales, or persons, living or dead, is coincidental.

Cover Design: www.mariahsinclair.com

---

1. http://www.gailmeath.com

Hollywood Quotes

"I don't want to fit in. I want to stand out and be remembered." - **Carole Lombard**

"I was born at the age of twelve on an MGM lot." - **Judy Garland**

"I'm not funny. What I am is brave." - **Lucille Ball**

"You only live once, but if you do it right, once is enough." - **Mae West**

"Life would be so wonderful if we only knew what to do with it." - **Greta Garbo**

"In Hollywood, brides keep the bouquets and throw away the groom." - **Groucho Marx**

"I'm just a lucky slob from Ohio who happened to be in the right place at the right time." - **Clark Gable**

1

October 19, 1937

A footstep out of rhythm.

That's what caught Vivian's attention as she and her husband, George, strolled down Hollywood Boulevard. She stopped dead in her tracks and glanced behind them. Crowds of people flooded the sidewalk, talking, laughing, and enjoying the unseasonably warm temperatures, and the streets were congested with traffic. Yet, the flat-footed *thud* of that single footstep had crawled up Vivian's spine.

"Is something wrong, darling?" George asked.

She turned to him. "I just caught a chill."

He wrapped his arm around her shoulders. "Better?"

Vivian smiled, and they continued walking. "David called a few minutes before you got home today. I asked him about the house for sale in Glendale, and it's still available. It might be small, George, but I loved the kitchen and thought it was perfect for us."

"I was hoping we'd find something larger, but if you have your heart set on it, I'll talk to Dave about it in the morning and make an offer."

"That's wonderful. I can't wait to have a home of our own in a nice, quiet neighborhood. The first thing I'm going to do is plant a flower garden out front."

"How is the new assistant working out at your fashion boutique?" George asked. "You haven't mentioned her lately."

"Nora? I'd be lost without her. At first, I worried she was too young and inexperienced, but she's a quick learner, and the customers adore her. I do, too. We've been experimenting with bolder colors and fashion designs that appeal to the younger crowd, and already, it's boosting business."

"I'm glad you found someone to replace your sister. You were working too many hours."

As they walked by the shoe store, Vivian pulled away from George and hurried over to the display window to read the sign. "Rats! They're sold out of the silver Ghillie lace sandals I've been eyeing, the ones I showed to you last evening. I was waiting for them to go on sale."

"You have plenty of shoes, darling. Our closet is overflowing with them."

"No, it's not. You're exaggerating. Besides, I save a lot of money making my own clothes. I'm entitled to a little indulgence." But she saw the smile on George's face, and her blue eyes lit up excitedly, thinking he'd purchased the shoes for her as an anniversary gift. She rushed to his side and took his arm again. "I'm looking forward to Saturday night even more now. Can you believe we've been married for an entire year already? Carole and Clark want to celebrate with us. They're going to meet us at Perino's Restaurant for dinner."

George stopped walking. "Don't you have an important fashion show at the Biltmore Hotel this weekend?"

"Yes, but it's only from ten o'clock to four on both days. I'm free on Saturday night. What's wrong, George?"

"Well, now I feel terrible. I thought you were busy all weekend, so I agreed to travel to our new bank facility in Sacramento to train the manager there. I'm leaving Friday morning and won't be back until Sunday afternoon. If I could get out of it, I would, but all the travel and hotel arrangements have been made. The bank also provided me with a sizeable bonus for the trip. I'll tell you what. Why don't we celebrate at Perino's on Thursday night instead? I'm sure Carole and Clark won't mind changing the date."

Vivian fell silent, unable to hide her disappointment.

George leaned over and kissed her. "I'm sorry for the mix-up, sweetheart. I promise to make it up to you. Let me grab a pack of cigarettes at the drugstore, and we'll go back to our apartment. I'll open a bottle of your favorite wine, and we can start celebrating our anniversary tonight. How does that sound?"

"That would be nice." She forced a smile, and he left her side.

As Vivian stood there waiting for him, she glanced up. Far above the bright neon store signs and streetlights lining both sides of the road, the full moon had turned a deep shade of burnt orange and glowed like a gem against the dark sky. Gazing at it, she recalled all the crazy ancient myths she'd heard about the *Blood Moon*, everything from it causing blindness to signifying the end of the world. She wondered how something so dazzling could gain such a bad reputation.

Vivian's entire body jerked with the sound of a single gunshot. She swung around and through the store window, she saw a man dressed in black pointing a gun at George. Before she could react, he pulled the trigger. She screamed George's name, but the shock of it kept her frozen in the spot until the gunman burst out the door and fled down the sidewalk.

Vivian ran into the drugstore and caught herself at the doorway. The bloody scene sickened her, but she fell to her knees beside George, lying on the floor. Quickly, she pulled her sweater off her shoulders, rolled it up into a ball, and pressed it over the bullet wound in his chest, trying to stop the bleeding. All the while, she was crying and calling his name over and over again.

Even after the police arrived, she refused to leave George's side, but an officer finally spoke to her softly, wrapped a comforting arm around her, and escorted her outside.

And that damn orange moon grabbed her attention again.

2

Tip-Off

Six Months Later: Saturday, April 30

Vivian remained hidden within the nighttime shadows of the tenant building on Hill Street, not far from Angel's Flight, the narrow funicular railway that carried passengers to the top and bottom of Bunker Hill. Her tailored suede hat was tipped low over her brows, and her hands were tucked deep into the side pockets of her oversized beige trench coat.

Tonight, her husband's death would finally be avenged.

Like clockwork, the two clanging railway cars began their trek on the steep hill, heading in opposite directions. As they passed by one another halfway on the hill, their headlights lit up the area for a few seconds and flashed in Vivian's blue eyes. Quickly, she lowered her head and pressed her back against the brick wall behind her until the noise faded and darkness concealed her again.

At one time not too long ago, Bunker Hill had separated the richest residents living in their grand Victorian mansions from the western end of the city. After the construction of nearby freeways, the wealthy fled to more elite neighborhoods like Beverly Hills and Pasadena, and Bunker Hill turned into one of the most populated and crime-laden neighborhoods in southern California, rivaled only by Skid Row.

Vivian stood there unbothered by the shady characters wandering about, the rowdy gang of teenagers gathered in front of the tavern down the road, or the quarreling couple shouting obscenities at one another from the open window above her. It wasn't the first time she'd been in a precarious situation, but hopefully, it would be the last.

She glanced up at the dark sky. There was a full moon, but tonight it shined pure white and crystal clear. Vivian tore her gaze away and focused on the two unmarked black sedans parked at either end of the block across the street from her.

Uneven footsteps alerted her to Lucky's approach, and she moved forward to greet him. The young man emerged from the darkness, walking with a slight limp. He wore jeans and a flannel shirt with his sleeves rolled up, accenting his broad shoulders and bulging biceps.

"Hey, blondie, how are you doing?"

"I have your cash, Lucky. I hope your information is solid."

"Solid as a rock. It's going down in a few minutes. Are you sure you want to stick around for it?"

Vivian wouldn't miss this for all the world. "I'm sure."

She held out the envelope of cash to him, but he just grinned at her. "Put your money away. We'll all rest a little easier when Kimball is behind bars."

"Take it, Lucky. I'm grateful for all your help."

He finally relented and stuck the envelope into his shirt pocket. "Thanks. We make a pretty good team, don't we? I tipped you off about this meeting and, in turn, you tipped off the cops. Let's just hope they don't screw it up." Lucky suddenly pushed Vivian back against the wall like a protective parent, and he went with her into the shadows, out of sight. "Kimball just walked out of the alley across the street. Here we go, Blondie."

A cold, morbid chill ran down Vivian's spine when she caught sight of the man who had taken her husband from her and destroyed their future together. She glared at him as he strolled over to the lamppost, leaned against it, and lit a cigarette.

He appeared so casual standing there, as though he didn't have a care in the world. As though he wasn't a cold-blooded murderer. His black hair was slicked back, his sun-leathered skin aged him well beyond his thirty-five years, and even at this distance, she could see the sunken pits on his cheeks, scars from a childhood bout of chicken pox.

She never got a look at his ugly face that fateful night. The swine had slithered past her on the sidewalk and followed George inside the drugstore. It wasn't until the police questioned a few witnesses afterward that they learned the killer's identity, but Elliott Kimball seemed to have vanished into thin air. So, the police gave up the search. They labeled the *burglary-gone-bad* case unresolved and filed it away.

That's when Vivian began an investigation of her own.

Easily, she discovered Kimball had plenty of petty arrests under his belt, and he was questioned as a suspect in mob-related murders twice, but he never spent any significant time in jail. He was just a two-bit hoodlum working by himself, and that made his trail even harder to follow.

When all was said and done, she'd risked much more than time and money trying to find him. Four months into it, she became so frustrated she finally resorted to pulling some strings from her past that she knew she'd regret. It also led her to Lucky, who assured her that they had something significant in their favor. Kimball was loathed more than liked by those who knew him, and that ended up being the key to finding him.

Lucky gently nudged her and pointed to another man across the street as he approached Kimball. They watched the two men chat briefly and head down the sidewalk together.

With perfect timing, the officers in the black sedans flicked on their high beams and sirens and sped toward them. Kimball and the other man panicked, pulled out their guns, and started shooting while they ran in different directions. But the unmarked cars came to a screeching halt on the sidewalk, trapping them both in front of several closed shops with no escape.

"Drop your weapons!" an officer shouted from the car.

Vivian glued her eyes on Kimball, who kept glancing at the alleyway not too far from him, as though debating whether he could make it around the police car without getting shot.

"I said, drop your weapons and put your hands in the air now!" the officer ordered.

In a flash, Kimball lifted his gun, pulled the trigger, and sent a sharp-shooting bullet through the sedan windshield, shattering the glass, and striking the officer in the driver's seat. Then Kimball made a run for it.

Vivian watched the scene intently as the other officers furiously opened fire. At the same time, a squad of police officers rushed out from the shadows and swarmed the area, blocking her view. She moved toward the road, desperately wanting to see the outcome, but Lucky grabbed her arm and held her back.

"Stay out of sight, Blondie. It's safer for you if the cops don't know you tipped them off."

She stood on her tiptoes, trying to see. "Did they catch him?"

"Yeah, I'd say so. They put enough bullets in him to kill an elephant. He obviously preferred death to life in prison."

Vivian pulled her arm free from Lucky's grip and fell back against the brick wall, closing her eyes. She couldn't believe it was over with just like that. After all her tears and hard work, a man she hated was dead. Truthfully, she was hoping Kimball would give himself up and spend the rest of his days behind bars, suffering every single moment for what he'd done.

Then again, his death was the closure she needed to move forward.

"Come on, Blondie, I'll buy you a glass of bourbon," Lucky told her. "I think we both could use a good, stiff drink."

But Vivian's eyes suddenly popped open. Something was wrong. Along with her artistic talent, she also possessed what some people considered a photographic memory, which is why her charcoal sketches of people, places, and events contained the most precise details, even after glimpsing the subjects of her drawings for only a moment.

Tonight, Elliott Kimball pulled his gun out of his right pocket and used his right hand to shoot back at the police. The man who killed George was holding the gun in his left hand.

3

Red Roses

Monday, May 2

"One more lap to go!" Carole called out as she and Vivian reached the deep end of her swimming pool. "Catch me if you can!" And she swam off.

Vivian took a deep breath, planted the bottoms of her feet against the side of the pool, and gave herself a good push using every bit of leg strength she had. She started swimming the breaststroke but switched to the front crawl, her fastest style, determined to beat Carole, for once. After twenty-nine laps, the two of them were nearly neck-in-neck heading into the shallow end, but after another ten seconds, Carole reached up and grabbed the edge of the pool just moments before Vivian.

"Rats! One of these days, Carole..." Vivian choked out as she leaned over the edge, trying to catch her breath while laughing at the same time.

Carole patted her on the back. "You're damn good, Viv, and you almost beat me this time. When you do, I'll give you one of my swimming trophies to take home with you. Come on, let's have some lemonade and dry off." They both lifted themselves out of the water, and Carole led the way to the patio table under the umbrella.

Vivian met Carole six years ago when she first moved to Los Angeles and worked for the costume designer at Paramount Pictures. Carole was filming the movie, *No Man of Her Own,* with Clark Gable. Surprisingly, Vivian and Carole became instant friends despite their personality differences or, perhaps, because of it. Vivian was new to the area, quieter, and preferred keeping a low profile. Carole, on the other hand, was outgoing, witty, and honest to a fault.

At the time, they were both twenty-four years old, and Carole not only introduced her to many influential people, but she also encouraged Vivian to open her fashion boutique right around the corner from Carole's home in Beverly Hills.

After Vivian threw her terrycloth robe on, she fell into the chair and smiled seeing Bella, her six-month-old Boston Terrier, and Carole's two-year-old dachshund, Tricksy, stretched out and sleeping together on a soft blanket under their own miniature umbrella stuck into the ground next to the table.

"I stopped by to see you and take a break from work, Carole," Vivian told her. "Now I'm exhausted!"

"Competition is good for the soul, and we always have a ton of fun. Right now, I'm the queen of the pool. You're tops in tennis, and we're even-steven in volleyball. Remember the time we played volleyball against my two brothers, and we won four out of five games? Charlie quit and refused to play with us anymore."

"Poor Charlie," Vivian snickered. "In his defense, he'd never played the game before."

"Even so, he should have been a better sport about it." Carole poured them both a glass of lemonade from the pitcher. "The story about Elliott Kimball made the front page of the Los Angeles Times." She slid the newspaper over to Vivian. "I'm mad at you for going to Bunker Hill without me. That's a dangerous place now. I don't know what you were thinking."

"I didn't want to put you in the middle of it."

"Why the hell not? You were there for me when Russ was killed four years ago. The two situations aren't that different, you know. I still don't think Russ' death was an accident. Before he picked me up for dinner, he stopped over at his good friend Lansing's house, and he wound up dead. Lansing claims he was *absentmindedly fooling around* with one of his firearms when it suddenly went off. Who on earth absentmindedly fools around with any gun?"

"I'm sorry you had to go through that, Carole. Russ was such a talented man. He wrote so many beautiful ballads."

"Well, it's in the past. My point is, I know what you're going through, and I give you great credit for trying so hard to find the culprit. Next time, please promise me that you'll tell me everything and include me in it instead of going off on your own."

"I promise, but a lot of good it did me. I was tracking the wrong man." Vivian skimmed through the newspaper article. "Oh dear, the officer in the unmarked car died."

"They also closed George's case, Viv. You need to tell the police about what you saw."

"What's the point?" She set the newspaper down and sipped her drink. "They weren't willing to search for Kimball when they had plenty of evidence for a conviction. If I told them that he didn't kill George, I doubt they'd be willing to start from scratch looking for who did."

"It's possible that Elliott Kimball was guilty. Maybe he was able to use his right and left hands equally. My mother was born left-handed, but my grandmother forced her to use her right hand growing up. To this day, she can use both hands interchangeably."

Vivian didn't buy that theory for a second, but she didn't want to talk about it anymore. On top of everything else, she felt partly responsible for the officer's death since she had alerted the police to Elliott Kimball's whereabouts. "I heard from Becca last night. She's having such a wonderful visit with her grandparents in Dallas."

"You mean, *Rebecca*," Carole chuckled. "Doesn't Ruth hate it when people refer to her by her nickname?"

"Yes, I can't tell you how many times she's had to correct me."

"I find it strange that Ruth let her travel so far on a train by herself. She's only twelve years old, isn't she?"

Vivian smiled, thinking about her stepdaughter. "Becca didn't seem to mind. Her father's death hit her very hard, and I think the change of scenery is doing her some good. We're going to spend a day together when she gets home if Ruth permits it."

"I don't understand why Ruth gives you such a hard time. She was the one who filed for divorce and pushed it through long before you came into the picture."

"I'm sure it's because George and I were only married for a short time, and now that he's gone, she doesn't think I should have anything to do with her daughter."

They heard a car door shut, and Carole slid back into her seat. "You'll never guess who invited I over for tea."

"Who?"

"Louella Parsons, the gossip columnist queen. She's dying to know the status of my relationship with Clark and has been driving us both nuts. She planted informants everywhere, in the studios, my hair salon, and even our doctors' offices, so I finally relented. I told Clark to steer clear until she left. I figured the best way to get her off our backs was to confront her directly."

"Be careful, Carole. Remember what happened to Mary Pickford? She let it slip to Louella that she and Douglas Fairbanks were contemplating divorce. Louella promised to keep it to herself, but the very next day, the news spread like wildfire."

"I know, but years ago my mother asked Louella to set up a screen test for me with Fox Film, and I nabbed the contract with them. The witch has never let my mother forget that we owe her a favor. So, I plan on giving her a nice, juicy scoop, but it won't be the one she's expecting."

"Whatever you say to her, please try to curb your tongue. It won't do your wholesome image any good if she includes some of your foul language in her column."

"To hell with my image!" Carole spat. "Maybe a little profanity will chase her away."

"That's got to be my little sister cursing like a sailor again," John laughed as he approached them. He leaned down and kissed Carole on the forehead. "Who's the brunt of your wrath this time?"

"Luckily, not me," Vivian chuckled. "How are you, John?"

"It's good to see you again, Vivian. I didn't see your car out front."

"I told her to park in the carport," Carole said. "That way, she can make a quick getaway when Louella Parsons arrives."

"Louella is coming here? So, that's who you were talking about. Then I gather Clark isn't around. I wanted to see if he was free to play a round of golf tomorrow."

"He'll be home in a couple of hours, John. I'm sure he'd love to."

Vivian stood up. "I think I'll leave before the *witch* gets here. She doesn't know me from a bag of beans, and I'd rather keep it that way."

"Why don't you join Clark and me for dinner this evening?" Carole asked. "Martha is making poached halibut and her infamous apple pudding."

"I wish I could, but I'm so backed up with orders, I'll probably be working through dinner. Oh, I forgot to mention that I'm nearly finished with the alterations on your satin beach pajamas. I made the trousers slightly wider than you normally wear, but it's all the rage now. I can deliver them to you tomorrow."

"Let me swing by and pick them up. I don't need them until the garden party I'm having here on Thursday, and I have a ton of errands to run before then. You're coming to it, aren't you?"

Vivian grabbed her towel. "I wouldn't miss it."

"It starts at four o'clock. Make sure you bring Bella with you. Gloria's daughter, Suzanne, offered to watch both her and Tricksy. I'm going to set up a little indoor play yard for them, so they don't get trampled on by the crowd of guests."

"Bella would like that."

Carole eyed her. "I know you too well, Viv. I see that look on your face, and I can almost hear your mind spinning with ideas. Don't you dare do anything else foolish, at least not without me."

She went over and hugged Carole. "We'll talk later. I'll see you on Thursday, John. Come along, Bella. Time to go home."

After Vivian changed into her lavender suit jacket and skirt in the bathhouse, she and Bella walked to the carport. Vivian tossed her swim bag in the back seat of her convertible Renault and lifted Bella into the passenger seat. Then she drove southeast toward downtown Los Angeles instead of heading directly to her boutique.

The breeze tousled her chin-length blonde curls and filled her lungs with fresh air. It felt as exhilarating as her dip in the pool, although Carole was right. Her mind was spinning with ideas, or maybe schemes, as she struggled to determine her next steps in finding out who murdered George.

After what happened at Bunker Hill, it crossed her mind that the whole incident at the drugstore might not have been a random hold-up. She never considered inquiring about the owner who also died that night. Perhaps he was the gunman's target, and poor George was just in the wrong place at the wrong time. Then there were the two witnesses who had claimed they got a good look at Kimball running out of the store. It would be worth her while to ask them a few questions now.

A car horn honked behind her, and Bella barked. Vivian noticed the traffic light had turned green and stepped on the gas. As she drove down the road, she looked in the rearview mirror.

A man driving a fancy sports car was right on her bumper, and so close she had half a mind to tap on the brakes to get him to back off. Then she worried he might be drunk and crash into her. So, she eventually slowed down, pulled over to the right side of the road, and waved him on.

Impatiently, he downshifted his car into second gear and revved his motor, then both he and the young woman in the passenger seat laughed as the red Jaguar sped around her. He tooted his horn again, and the woman yelled, "Toodle-oo, honey!"

Vivian recognized both the car and the driver. "Preston Stone...it figures." She rolled her eyes and continued driving.

Along the way, she stopped to pick up a bouquet of daisies at the florist shop, and upon reaching her destination, she parked in the grass alongside the tall wrought-iron fence surrounding Evergreen Cemetery. She carried the flowers with her, and she and Bella strolled through the open gates.

The groundskeeper was trimming the hedgerow by the stone chapel and tipped his hat in greeting. Bella started growling at him since she didn't trust strangers, but Vivian hushed her and wished the groundskeeper a good day. She could hear the chirping goldfinch and warblers even before she saw them fluttering from branch to branch in the orchid tree beside George's grave.

She stopped short several feet away.

There were at least two dozen fresh-cut red roses wrapped in a wide pink ribbon lying on the ground beside the engraved granite stone.

Bella went over and sniffed the roses while Vivian glanced around the cemetery. There was only one other person in sight besides the groundskeeper. A gentleman was standing beside another grave a distance away with his head held down and his hands folded in front of him.

Vivian looked at the red roses again and couldn't imagine who left them here. No one ever had before, except for Becca, but she'd been out of town for the past week. Certainly, Ruth wouldn't have made the trip from Encino all by herself. At the funeral, she'd made it known that she only attended for her daughter's sake.

Hesitantly, Vivian moved forward, staring at the red roses. She bent down to place her daisies on the other side of the stone and said a silent prayer. Then she closed her eyes and tipped her head back.

"The witnesses were sure Elliott Kimball ran from the store that night, George, but they were wrong. It wasn't him. I don't know how I'm going to do it, but I promise you, I won't rest until I find out who pulled that trigger."

She swallowed hard and looked down at the grave, but all she saw were the red roses.

4

Anonymous

It was close to four o'clock when Vivian pulled into the side alley between her building and Martino's Delicatessen. She got out of her car and decided to walk around the front of the boutique with Bella instead of going through the side door so she could take another look at their new window display of summer dresses and casual outfits.

As they approached the front door, Vivian could hear the radio inside playing loud and clear, and Nora was singing right along with Kenny Baker, the popular heartthrob singer. Vivian peeked into the front window. Nora was wearing one of her designs, a bright yellow floral dress with a flair skirt, and she was dancing and twirling around the room while dusting the shelves and straightening the clothes hanging on the display racks.

Vivian smiled and opened the door. The bell jingled. Immediately, Nora rushed over to turn the music down, thinking she was a customer. "Vivian! I'm so glad you're back. We had eight walk-in sales while you were gone, and the telephone has been ringing off the hook."

She lifted a brow. "I'm surprised you could hear the phone with both you and Kenny Baker crooning away together?"

Nora's face turned beet red.

Vivian laughed. "That's all right. The customers enjoy listening to music while they shop here. It fits the ambiance, but let's keep the volume down just a bit." They walked into the back room. "Were there any messages?"

"Yes, three of them."

Vivian took the list from her. "Gary Rutherford called? What did he say?"

"He wanted you to call his office as soon as you returned. I wrote the telephone number down. Who is he?"

Vivian stared at the message. "I met him at the fashion show we had on Friday at the Biltmore Hotel. He's a wholesale buyer for Bullock's department store, and we talked for quite a while. He seemed impressed with my designs and said he'd be in touch with me. So far, our clientele only consists of individual customers. I always dreamed of snaring a department store contract."

"Bullock's is the biggest department store on the west coast! That would be fantastic."

Vivian took a deep breath, picked up the receiver, and dialed the number, but it just kept ringing. "There's no answer."

"He sounded anxious to speak with you when he called," Nora told her. "I'm sure he has good news. All my friends are shopping here now. We all agree that your designs are fabulous, far better than any of the department stores in the area, even Bullock's."

"You're very sweet, Nora."

"Oh, a messenger also delivered this to you while you were out. It looks like a formal invitation."

Vivian took the envelope from her. *Missus George Ramsey* was typed on the front of it, which she found odd. Few people had ever referred to her by that title since she never changed her name after she got married. George had advised her against it for business purposes.

She picked up the letter opener on the table and carefully slid it under the flap of the envelope. Inside, there was a note stating, *'You are cordially invited.'* She pulled out the single movie ticket. "It's admission for a movie premiere at the Liberty Theatre Wednesday afternoon."

"What movie?" Nora asked.

"It doesn't say." She flipped it over. "I have no idea who sent this."

"Maybe it's from Olivia De Havilland. Last Tuesday, she told us about her new movie coming to theaters this weekend, *The Adventures of Robin Hood*. It stars Errol Flynn, and he's such a dreamboat."

"I remember her talking about it." Vivian looked at the envelope again. "You enjoy going to the movies more than I do. Why don't you take this?"

"I don't think I should," Nora said. "It's the premiere, and Miss De Havilland will probably be at the theater expecting to see you. Like you always say, it's all about good customer relations. Besides, my friends and I have been dying to see it, and we already made plans to go this weekend."

Vivian set the envelope aside. "I'll think about it. You've been working since early this morning, Nora. Why don't you head home now? I can handle things from here."

"Too late. I wasn't sure if you had a chance to stop for lunch, so I ordered two chicken caprese sandwiches for us for dinner." Nora took the ironing board out of the closet and set it up. "Tony Martino is going to deliver them in about half an hour. I have plenty to do while we wait."

"Thank you, Nora. I'm going to drop my swim bag off upstairs and fix Bella some dinner." She looked at Bella, sitting at her feet. "Stay with Nora. I'll be right back."

Vivian climbed the stairs to her apartment, which spanned the entire second floor of the two-story building she had rented for her business. She unlocked the door and set her purse on the end table next to her wedding picture. After gazing at the photograph for a moment, she reached over and ran her fingertips along the thick brass frame.

She and George met two years ago at a holiday party hosted by Barney Balaban, president of Paramount Pictures. She had left the company but decided to go with a few associates she'd remained friends with, and George had just been promoted to manager of Bank of America, where Mister Balaban had several accounts.

George wasted no time introducing himself to her. He was sweet and charming and swept her off her feet. She was also struck by his sincerity, openly telling her about his divorce a few years earlier, and he spoke so lovingly of his nine-year-old daughter. Five months later, they were married in a small church with only a few close friends.

Then it all came crashing down around her the night he died. Vivian didn't want to give up her search for the man responsible for his death, but she was growing tired. She'd spent so much time and energy doing exactly that, and where did it get her? Now, the task seemed near impossible. She needed to start from scratch without any viable witnesses or any type of evidence at all that might steer her in the right direction.

Vivian finally walked down the hallway and set her swim bag down on the chair in her bedroom. Then she went into the kitchen to cut up small chunks of fresh turkey breast for Bella. When she finished, she took the small dish downstairs and put it on the floor beside Bella's bowl of water. She noticed a stack of shoeboxes in the corner.

"Where did those boxes come from?"

Nora set the iron down. "Henry stopped by about an hour ago and delivered the shoes for us to take to the public market. I told him that we didn't need them until Wednesday morning, but he said his father wanted to get them off the shelves at their store to make room for a new shipment."

Vivian chuckled. "Henry will use any excuse to see you. He's terribly smitten with you, Nora. That's the only reason they agreed to donate two dozen kilties and oxfords for the market. That reminds me. Let's not forget to bring the boxes of accessories with us when we go there."

"They're on my list." The telephone rang, and Nora hurried over to answer it. "Good afternoon, Vivian's Boutique. How can I help you? May I ask who's calling? One moment, please. I'll see if she's available." Nora covered the mouthpiece. "Vivian, the woman refuses to give me her name, but she said she needs to speak with you right away. She sounds pretty upset. What should I do?"

"I'll talk to her." Vivian took the receiver. "Hello, this is Vivian Steele." As she listened to the woman on the other end, she turned her back to Nora and lowered her voice. "What type of information? Yes, I know where it is. I understand, but you need to tell me what this is about first."

The woman hung up.

Vivian held onto the receiver a moment longer before slowly setting it down on the base. She wasn't sure if it was the woman's obscurity or the tone of her voice, but she had a bad feeling about this.

"Who was it?" Nora asked.

"I...I need to go out again for a bit. Do you mind?"

"No, not at all."

Vivian noticed Bella was already curled up and sleeping in her bed. "Can I leave Bella with you, too? She's had a busy day. She'll probably sleep until I get back."

"That's fine, Vivian. I'll take care of her. Can I do anything else for you?"

"Make sure you charge the sandwiches to my account and start without me, but I shouldn't be long." She ignored the worried look on Nora's face and made her way out the front door.

5

Beverly Hills Hotel

Vivian pulled into the parking lot at the Beverly Hills Hotel, the ritzy pink stucco building that was surrounded by acres of beautiful gardens on Sunset Boulevard. She turned her car off and sat there, debating what to do.

The woman on the telephone didn't give her any reason at all to think that the information she had pertained to George's murder. She made that assumption all on her own since it was all she thought about these days. Yet, she couldn't imagine what else would be so secretive that the woman insisted upon meeting in person.

Vivian snatched her handbag and got out of the car. After she walked across the parking lot, an elderly man in uniform greeted her and opened the front door for her. Inside the beautiful, spacious lobby, a handful of people were sitting on the sofa and others relaxed in the wingback chairs, reading the newspaper or waiting for their companions.

That's when Vivian caught sight of Preston Stone and cursed under her breath. He was leaning over the front desk, flirting with the pretty redheaded clerk. She wanted to avoid him like the plague, and thankfully, the mysterious woman on the phone had given her the room number. So, she walked over to the far wall, making a wide half-circle around the front desk until she stood in front of the elevator down a short corridor.

Vivian pressed the 'up' button and tapped her foot impatiently while sneaking a few peeks to make sure Preston didn't spot her. He was still busy sweet-talking the poor young lady behind the counter. Finally, the elevator doors opened. Two people got off, and she stepped inside. She pushed the fourth-floor button. It was a good minute before the doors began closing, and she breathed a sigh of relief.

But just before the doors touched, a large hand slid in between, stopping them. The doors slowly opened again, and Preston Stone stood there with an annoying twinkle in his dark eyes and his lips curled up into a pompous grin.

"Hello, Vivian. You're looking well."

She nodded her head in return and moved to one side of the elevator.

He got on and deliberately stood in the center. "How is business at your fashion boutique?"

She glared at him. "I don't see any reason for us to make small talk."

He tipped his head sideways, pretending to look hurt. "I was hoping after all this time we could bury the hatchet. It's been close to a year now, hasn't it? I admit I behaved badly."

Vivian thanked the powers above that the doors finally closed, and the elevator started moving. "If that's an apology, I'm not the one you should be talking to."

His grin widened. "Does Patricia still work at your shop?"

"No, after you broke my sister's heart, she moved to the east coast."

"Aw, poor kid. Well, in my defense, I told her straight up that I wasn't the type to settle down."

Ooh, he really got under her skin. "Don't worry your swelled head about it, Preston. You didn't scar her for life. She's already engaged to a wealthy stockbroker."

"Good for her! See? Sounds like she let bygones be bygones. I think you should, too, Vivian. After all, I didn't break your heart...did I?"

If she were a man, he'd be lying on the floor right now with a black eye.

Luckily, the elevator slowed to a stop on the fourth floor. The bell rang once, and Vivian impatiently waited for the doors to open just far enough for her to slip through them. Once done, she saw the small sign hanging on the wall that gave the direction of the room numbers, and she quickly headed down the hall to her left.

She heard someone walking behind her and glanced around. Preston had gotten off the elevator, too, and he was trailing her. She picked up her pace. "Don't you have anything better to do than follow me?"

He chuckled. "As much as I enjoy sparring with you, it just so happens that I'm meeting someone who is staying on this floor."

Vivian reached room Forty-Four and waited for Preston to pass by her before she knocked on the door. Instead, he ended up standing beside her. She let out an exasperated groan. "What are you doing, Preston?"

"Okay, now I have to agree with you that this is a little awkward. The person I'm meeting is staying in room Forty-Four."

Vivian flashed her eyes at him. "You're kidding me?"

"I wish I was," he said. "I'll let you have the honor of knocking on the door."

She had half a mind to walk away and forget about all this, but she was even more curious than before. She lifted her hand and knocked.

The door fell open.

They both stood there silently. Vivian was hoping Preston would call to the woman since she had no idea what her name was, but he looked at her as though waiting for her to make the first move.

"Hello?" she finally said.

Dead silence.

Vivian stepped away from the door. "Apparently, she's not home."

"Hold on." Preston pushed the door all the way open and walked into the foyer. "Stay here, Vivian. I'm going to take a look around."

She resented him telling her what to do, so she followed him inside. They made their way down a short hall, and Vivian could see the living area that was elegantly furnished with twin Queen Anne wingback chairs and a matching velvet sofa.

Preston suddenly stopped dead in his tracks. "Son of a gun..."

Vivian gasped when she noticed the blonde woman sprawled on the floor in front of the wooden coffee table with blood saturating her white blouse.

Preston hurried over, got on one knee, and pressed his fingers against the woman's neck. "She's dead. Looks like a gunshot to her chest."

It took Vivian a second to grasp what he'd said. During that moment, she spotted a framed photograph propped on the coffee table. Frowning, she moved closer to get a better look, and her heart sank. It was a picture of George and the dead woman on a boat, arm-in-arm, like lovers.

Her vision darted to the woman lying on the floor again, and she groaned out loud.

"Are you okay, Vivian?" Preston asked.

She covered her mouth and nodded her head almost frantically, glad that he thought it was seeing the dead woman that upset her. But she just noticed the woman's shoes. They were silver Ghillie lace sandals, exactly like the pair she thought George had bought for her as an anniversary gift. It never occurred to her that she never found those shoes among his things after his death.

"Well, this poses a bit of a problem," Preston said. "Did you know her very well?"

Vivian hesitated, trying to find her voice as well as an excuse for being here. "She...she was a potential client and wanted to meet this afternoon to hear more about my services. I just spoke with her no more than twenty minutes ago. What about you?"

He didn't answer her right away, either. "I met her at a party over the weekend, and we had a dinner date tonight."

Vivian had the feeling that he didn't believe her any more than she believed him, but right now, she was more interested in distracting him so she could take the photograph. "Really? What was her name, Preston?"

"Okay, now you're being childish, Vivian. Neither one of us had anything to do with her death."

"I know I didn't," she told him.

"I'll tell you what. Why don't we go our separate ways and let the hotel take care of this? Otherwise, we'll both be stuck for hours in red tape. The police will take us down to the station, and we'll spend the night answering a lot of ridiculous questions until they exhaust the issue."

As he spoke, he walked over to look out the window. Vivian snatched the photograph and hid it behind her back. "I hate to say it, but I agree with you."

"There's a stairway at the end of the hall. Why don't you take that down to the first floor instead of the elevator? It leads to the back lot outside."

"All right." Vivian looked at the woman again. Under different circumstances, she wouldn't dream of just leaving without calling the police or, at the very least, alerting the hotel manager. Normally, she would feel far more grief and compassion for the woman lying there and question why Preston was so quick to suggest they sneak away.

Instead, she headed straight for the door without another word while slipping the photograph into her handbag.

"See you around, Vivian!"

She ignored him and walked down the hall to the stairway. When she was outside, she headed to the parking lot and got into her car. She sat there for a moment, staring at her handbag before driving back to the boutique.

Nora was waiting for her with the sandwiches she'd ordered. Vivian didn't know how she managed it, but after she assured Nora that everything was fine, the two of them sat at the table in the back room, chatting and eating their meal. Another hour passed before Nora finally headed home.

As soon as she left, Vivian locked the front door, and she and Bella went upstairs to her apartment. Vivian set her handbag down on the kitchen counter and immediately took the photograph out. Her stomach turned when she glimpsed the photo again. She flipped it over and using the seam ripper from the sewing pouch in her purse, she bent the four picture points that held the cardboard in place. She removed the photo and looked at the back of it.

As she suspected, it was dated the last weekend in September of last year when George had supposedly traveled to San Diego on business. Without hesitation, she grabbed the telephone receiver on the counter and dialed zero.

"Hello, operator, could you give me the number for the Sacramento branch of the Bank of America, please?" She opened the drawer and pulled out a piece of paper and pen to write the information down. "Excuse me? Are you sure? Okay, thank you." She slammed the receiver down.

The bank didn't have a branch in Sacramento. George had lied to her again and intended to spend their first anniversary with his mistress.

Dazed by it all, she went into the living room and sat on the sofa, petting Bella lying beside her and glaring at her wedding picture on the end table.

She'd thought the day she married George was the best day of her life. For years, she swore she would never get married or have children. She also had good reason for not trusting too many people, but when she met George, it felt good to let her guard down and not worry about the past anymore. She only wanted to look to the future with him and even hoped after they bought the house in Glendale, they might talk about starting a family of their own.

George had lied to her from the start. She didn't know him at all, but she sure as heck was going to find out all she could about his mistress, and why someone murdered her, too.

6

The Mistress

Tuesday, May 3

Vivian tossed and turned all night and got up at the crack of dawn. Then she sat at the kitchen table, fully dressed, drinking coffee, and staring at the photograph of George on the boat with his girlfriend. She had so many questions, but she didn't dare call the hotel or the police to find out some of the answers.

Instead, she'd turned on her Zenith radio to station KGFJ, one of the twenty-four-hour radio stations in Los Angeles, and the window was wide open so she could hear the newsboy across the street when he arrived with the morning edition of the L.A. Times.

First, she wanted to find out if and when someone had discovered the woman in the hotel room, and what the police knew about her death. Most importantly, she needed to know the woman's name. Only then could she start digging deeper into how George knew her, along with who had killed her.

She thanked her lucky stars that no one knew she'd gone to the hotel, except for Preston, but he had his own worries. He'd carried on quite a conversation with the desk clerk before going upstairs and goodness knows what he told her, or what she'd said to the police. Whereas Vivian had slipped up to the fourth floor and back down again unnoticed.

Of course, there was also a good possibility that Preston had something to do with the woman's death, and that was the reason he'd rushed her out the door so quickly. She didn't trust him as far as she could throw him. And in that case, she could have quite a bit to worry about.

Her ears perked up, listening to the news report on the radio. *"Tilly Trimble, a young and aspiring actress, was found dead in her room at the Beverly Hills Hotel yesterday. The police listed her death as a homicide. No arrests have been made at this time. Miss Trimble had starred in a few low-budget films, but according to her agent, he was currently negotiating a contract for her with MGM. If you have any information regarding her death, you can contact the police directly at..."*

She turned the radio off and glanced at the photo again. Then she leaned closer, scowling and squinting at the picture, looking at George's left hand gripping Tilly Trimble's waist. "You rat, George. You took your wedding band off. Did you tell her about me, or did you lie to her, too?" She tossed the picture aside. "Well, Tilly found out about me at some point."

Vivian remembered the red roses at the gravesite and realized Tilly had left them. And that raised another concern. Did the young woman keep any other mementos in her hotel room that linked her to George, additional photographs, love letters, or...some of his belongings? Not only would it be embarrassing if the police came calling to question her about her husband's affair, but they might even suspect her in Tilly's murder.

The telephone rang, startling her, and she hurried over to answer it. "Hello? Oh, hello, Mister Rutherford. I tried calling you back yesterday, but there was no answer. Yes, I'm free tomorrow. Brookdale Cafeteria at eleven-thirty. I'll bring my portfolio with me. Thank you very much."

Vivian stood there after she hung up. She should be ecstatic that the executives at Bullock's were anxious to see her portfolio. It meant her dream might finally come true, but she was such a bundle of emotions right now with anger overriding her glory. She dumped her coffee into the sink and went downstairs with Bella.

Nora arrived at eight-thirty and tossed her colorful beechwood beaded handbag on the table. "Good morning, Vivian! It's a beautiful day outside.

Here's the newspaper, and I bought bagels for us. My bus stop is directly in front of Loretta's Bakery, and they smelled too good to pass up. I'll make a pot of coffee."

"Thank you, Nora. That was thoughtful of you. Gary Rutherford called again. I'm meeting him for lunch tomorrow. He wants to show the executives my portfolio."

"Vivian, that's fantastic!"

"I don't want to get my hopes up." Vivian picked up the newspaper and flipped through it. "If it goes through, and they offer me a contract, we'll need to hire a salesclerk to take care of the walk-in customers. That way, you'll have more time to help me with the orders. We'll also have to do some renovating back here."

"My roommate, Nancy, works at the May Company. She has experience, and I know she would love to work here." Nora finished making a pot of coffee and glanced over Vivian's shoulder as she walked by. "Did you see the article about Tilly Trimble? It's such a shame, isn't it? She was only twenty-two years old, the same age as me. I saw two of her movies a while ago, and they were pretty corny. I hate to badmouth the dead, but I thought she stunk as an actress."

"I heard she was negotiating a contract with MGM," Vivian mentioned. "She must have had some talent."

"Well, it's not what you know, but who you know that counts. Her death didn't surprise me one bit." Nora headed for the doorway. "I'm going to straighten up the window display before we open the shop."

"Wait a minute, Nora. What do you mean, her death didn't surprise you?"

"It's all about the company you keep." When Vivian looked puzzled, Nora wandered over to her. "Jeepers, I thought everyone knew about Tilly's affair with Mayor Shaw. He's definitely not someone you want to cross. They say he's running all kinds of illegal businesses across the city, and he has the chief of police and a slew of other officers in his pocket. If Tilly broke up with him, or if his wife found out about her, it probably wouldn't be the first time he had someone eliminated to get rid of a problem."

Vivian made light of it. "I think you're watching too many movies, Nora."

"I'm just saying. I wasn't surprised when I heard she was murdered."

After Nora disappeared into the other room, Vivian poured herself a cup of coffee and sat down at the table. She'd heard plenty about the mayor's sordid reputation, too, and read about the car pipe bomb that had nearly killed Harry Raymond, a private detective and former police chief who was investigating the mayor and his associates. An intense trial was going on right now, charging an LAPD captain with attempted murder for planting the bomb.

Even if Nora was right about Tilly and the mayor, that might explain her death, but it didn't have anything to do with George's murder seven months ago. Not unless the young actress was seeing both men last fall, and the mayor found out about it.

Vivian stood up with goosebumps running up and down her arms. As much as she wanted to find out the truth about George's death despite his infidelity, pursuing Elliott Kimball was a walk in the park compared to the repercussions she could face trying to prove the mayor had something to do with it.

"Nora, could you come here for a minute?" she called out as she went over to pour herself another cup of coffee and one for Nora.

Nora poked her head into the back room. "What is it, Vivian?"

"The shop doesn't open for another half hour. Why don't we enjoy some coffee and a bagel before we unlock the doors?"

"Sounds good to me."

"I'm curious about what you said before. How did you hear about Tilly Trimble's affair with the mayor?"

Nora grabbed a bagel and handed the bag to Vivian. "Rumors have been flying around about it since last summer, but I saw them together, myself. It was at the premiere of one of Tilly's movies. They weren't holding hands or anything, but they were pretty snuggly after the lights went out."

"And you think he had her killed?"

Nora shrugged her shoulders. "You've read about the pipe bomb trial, haven't you? Captain Kynette of the LAPD is facing a lot of felony charges, but I bet he gets off. He's the mayor's right-hand man...or I should say, his henchman. A friend of mine told me that he did all the mayor's dirty work and his nickname on the streets is *Butcher*. That tells you a lot about the guy. It wouldn't surprise me if the mayor ordered him to kill Tilly."

As though the rest of it didn't matter, Vivian asked, "When did you see them together? Tilly and the mayor, I mean."

"Gosh, her movie came out a few weeks before Christmas. Like I said, the movie wasn't very good. The real entertainment was watching the two of them trying to act discreet." Nora took a bite of her bagel. "I feel bad for the mayor's wife. If she didn't know about their affair before, it's bound to make the headlines now."

Vivian sat upright. She just realized there were probably people who knew about George's affair with Tilly, too. He may not have had a lot of good friends, but he talked about a few of his co-workers at the bank. He also had three golfing buddies, including David, his best friend from college. David's wife called Vivian now and then, but other than that, she hadn't seen George's friends since his funeral.

She intended to contact them now. It seemed unlikely that Tilly owned the boat in the photograph, so it probably belonged to one of them.

At nine o'clock, Nora went into the display room to open the boutique. As soon as she left, Vivian glanced through the newspaper again and found the legal section. The trial was going to resume in an hour.

Captain Kynette piqued her curiosity now. From what Nora said, it was possible that he not only killed Tilly, but he was the gunman at the drugstore last fall and killed George, the mayor's romantic rival. She wanted to get a good look at the officer and hear more about the charges against him.

Vivian busied herself for the next half hour, then she gathered her handbag and told Nora that she had a few errands to run. She hated to leave Bella behind, but they didn't allow dogs in the courthouse.

She drove to the city, and the trial was already in progress by the time she entered the courtroom, which was full with standing room only. Vivian joined the spectators against the back wall and had a bird's-eye view of the prosecutor and defendant's table as well as the judge and witness box. And the prosecutor was questioning a witness now.

"Please describe the physical altercation that ensued after the defendant threatened your business partner," the prosecutor told the older gentleman on the stand.

The attorney jumped to his feet. "I object, your honor. Mister Kruger's testimony has no bearing on the charges against my client."

"I'm afraid it's quite relevant in establishing the defendant's pattern of using threats and violence," the prosecutor argued.

"I will allow it," the judge replied.

The prosecutor repeated the question. As the witness resumed testifying, Vivian watched Captain Kynette, dressed in a pristine suit and tie, lean over to speak with his attorney. She couldn't see him very clearly, so she made her way over to join the spectators standing along the far wall and inched herself closer to the front of the room.

As she stood there, she kept her eyes on the officer as he picked up a pen and scribbled something down on a pad. She didn't miss the fact that Captain Kynette was left-handed. He ripped the page off, folded it up, and turned around to hand it to the person sitting directly behind him.

Vivian took a step forward to see who received the note, and Joe Shaw, the mayor's brother and self-appointed chief of staff, was reading it. In the next second, he glanced over in her direction.

Quickly, she stepped back into the crowd.

"Can you tell us again when and where the incident took place, Mister Kruger?" the prosecutor asked.

"Yes, sir," the witness said. "It was the fifth of September on Labor Day weekend last year at our boat docks in Marina del Rey. The defendant had just finished tying off Mayor Shaw's wooden Chris-Craft boat in slip number twenty-two when he confronted my partner on the docks."

Vivian snapped her head up and stared at the witness. It seemed insane to think that George would sneak around with his girlfriend on the mayor's boat, but at this point, she wouldn't put any stupid decision past George. With a desperate need to know, she headed out of the courthouse and drove to Marina del Rey.

Thirty minutes later, she stood on the docks in front of the covered wooden boat at slip number twenty-two, gazing across the water at Ballona Bridge and the foothills in the distance, which was the same background scenery in the photograph.

All the pieces started falling into place.

If Tilly had just found out who killed George, that would explain everything, like why she left the red roses at the gravesite yesterday. It wasn't out of love and heartache. Otherwise, she would have left flowers at the cemetery long before this. It was out of guilt. Tilly discovered one of her lovers had arranged her other lover's murder.

It also seemed likely that guilt had driven Tilly to call her and insist they meet in her hotel room. According to Nora, Tilly had continued seeing the mayor after George died, so it was doubtful that the photograph had been sitting on her coffee table all this time. Rather, Tilly placed it there on purpose. She wanted Vivian to see it as soon as she arrived and intended to tell her about their affair.

But there had to be more to it than that. Tilly sounded upset on the phone, almost desperate. Did she also intend to tell her who murdered George?

As Vivian's thoughts frantically circled around, she wondered again why Preston showed up at Tilly's hotel room at the exact same time she did.

7

Stone

The Stone Estate was located in Santa Monica and sat on five acres of beachfront property. The ninety-two-room, thirty thousand square foot oceanfront mansion included three kitchens, twenty-six bedrooms, twelve fireplaces, a two-story library, four bars, outdoor tennis courts, guest houses, and an ornate swimming pool with a marble patio and two staircases.

Preston stood on the back terrace on the second floor of the south wing with his foot propped on the bottom rung of the railing. He gazed at the rolling ocean waves with his mind churning in rhythm. His thoughts kept bouncing back and forth from what he knew for a fact and his own observations.

"Excuse me, sir. Mister Frederick Barcroft just arrived," the butler announced. "Shall I show him in?"

Preston continued staring at the scenery. "For God's sake, Gunther, how many times do I have to tell you to stop calling me *sir*? Save your formalities for my father. And yes, please tell Freddie that I'm here on the terrace."

"Very well, sir."

Preston went back to his musings. Soon, he heard a faint commotion behind him. He turned around and saw Freddie standing by the liquor cart in the upstairs living room. "Did you have any trouble getting here?"

Freddy joined him outside. "Yeah, turn left and look for the biggest house on the beach. It was tough."

"I see you fixed yourself a drink."

"Hey, while you're basking here in luxury, I'm staying in some crummy motel on the strip. I think you can afford to buy me a Manhattan. This is one hell of a joint your parents have here." He walked over to the railing. "Your butler isn't a very friendly fella, though, is he? I thought he was going to frisk me before letting me inside."

"Gunther has been working here for over twenty years. He's very loyal, and frankly, I don't blame him, Freddie. That black pinstripe suit makes you look like a two-bit hoodlum."

Freddy primped up his collar. "I think it's pretty snazzy."

"You would." Preston glanced into the living room. "I'm surprised you didn't bring Boris with you."

"I did. He wanted to stretch his legs, so he's wandering around outside somewhere." Freddie leaned over the railing and pointed toward the beach. "There he is, heading straight for the water. Dang it, now he's going to get my truck seat all wet. I swear Boris isn't happy unless he's soaking wet or covered in mud."

Preston grinned as he watched the one hundred-and-sixty-pound Saint Bernard run into the bay and start frolicking in the waves along the shore. "I'll give you a couple of bath towels for him before you leave." He wandered over to the small table on the terrace and relaxed in one of the chairs. "What did you find out?"

Freddie set his drink on the table and sat down. "For starters, she left her shop around nine-thirty this morning and went straight to the courthouse. She watched the Kynette trial for about half an hour."

"The Kynette trial?" Preston asked as he sat down. "I wonder why."

"I don't know. I went inside the courtroom right behind her, but she just stood along the wall with all the other spectators. Then something the witness said caught her attention, and she couldn't get out of there fast enough."

"What did the witness say?"

"He was describing an incident that happened between his business partner and Kynette on the docks in Marina del Rey last August. And that's exactly where she went. She stood on those docks for the longest time right in front of the slip where the mayor keeps his boat."

Preston rested his elbows on the table and clasped his hands together, thinking about it. "Then what?"

"Afterwards, she drove here to Santa Monica and sat in her car in front of a small brick house on Pearl Street for about fifteen minutes. When an older man looked out the window, she drove off."

"She didn't go inside?"

"Nope."

"What was the number of the house?"

"Forty-eight." Freddie sipped his drink. "Whoever it belongs to takes really good care of their yard. It has a nice flower garden out front."

"All right. You never found out who was with her at Bunker Hill, did you?"

Freddie shook his head. "Like I said, he was a pretty slick fella. I lost his trail after the two of them left the tavern on Spring Street. I can keep looking for him if you want."

"Let it go for now. At least I know why she was there. Is there anything else?"

"That's about it. Since I was in the neighborhood, I figured I'd give you an update. Do you want me to keep following her?"

"Yes, and Freddie, in case you haven't heard. There's a newfangled contraption called a *telephone* that you can use to keep me updated. It's a heck of a lot easier and quicker."

Freddie laughed and gulped his drink down. "If it could make a Manhattan, I'd use it more often."

"Come on, let's go downstairs. I'm meeting Nick at the Bank of America at one o'clock, and it'll probably take us a while to drag Boris out of the water. I'll grab those towels."

"What's going on at the bank?"

"We're just gathering more information right now," Preston told him.

"Do you need my help?"

"No, we've got this covered, Freddie. Just keep an eye on Vivian and give me a call tomorrow."

By the time they got down to the beach, Boris was lounging in the waves about three feet offshore, soaked and loving every minute. Finally, they lured him away from the beach and dried him off. Freddie got Boris into the front seat of his rickety black Ford pickup truck parked out front, and they drove off.

Preston made his way back inside to his study on the second floor. He closed the door behind him and stood over his desk, staring at the papers and photographs spread across the top of it.

He couldn't be sure that Vivian's actions were unrelated to the Willoughby assignment, but it seemed unlikely. She seemed more focused on her husband's death, which is why she went to Bunker Hill to watch the police capture his killer, and yesterday, she only went to the hotel after she received the phone call from Miss Trimble requesting to meet with her.

Deliberately, Preston waited in the hotel lobby until Vivian arrived, and he got on the elevator with her. He honestly didn't expect her to treat him with such hostility after all this time. That's what drove him to follow her to Tilly's room, even though he'd never met Tilly and had no idea what he would have said had she answered the door.

He was surprised as hell to see Tilly lying dead on the floor, but Vivian was even more surprised to see the photograph on the coffee table. The minute she swiped it, he had a pretty good idea about what was going on.

He was also convinced that Vivian had absolutely nothing to do with Tilly's murder. Otherwise, she would have taken the other two pictures that were in plain sight and searched the rest of the apartment to remove all the evidence, like the shoebox full of love notes and photos of Tilly and Vivian's husband that he found underneath the bed.

Preston shuffled through the photographs he'd dumped onto his desk, some of which even made him blush. He picked up the one with Tilly and George Ramsey posing together on the Venice Beach Boardwalk and studied it. Then, he re-read the last note, or rather love letter, George had written to Tilly, which was dated the day he died.

Apparently, George and Tilly were planning to run away together that weekend.

Preston knew if the police had found the shoebox, they would immediately put Vivian at the top of their list of suspects in Tilly's murder. She might also be accused of hiring Elliott Kimball to kill her husband if someone on the police force had seen her at Bunker Hill watching the whole thing go down.

So, after he shooed her out of the hotel room, he packed up the other photographs, the shoebox, and the illegal wiretap that he had Freddie connect to Tilly's phone for an entirely different purpose and took everything with him. Then, just before he left the room, he discovered the bullet shell casing on the floor and deduced Tilly was shot with a thirty-eight-caliber Beretta handgun.

Now, along with everything else, he was curious to know why Tilly had a sudden urge to meet with her former lover's wife minutes before someone killed her.

The telephone on his desk rang, and Preston quickly picked it up. "Hello? What have you got, Barney? Nothing! Did you check the East Coast? Her sister, Patricia, moved there sometime last year. Are you sure you spelled their name correctly? There's an '*e*' at the end of Steele."

Preston got up from his chair and started pacing back and forth behind his desk while listening to Barney squawk. "Okay, okay, I understand. I didn't mean to yell at you. Just keep looking. There's got to be some sort of information about them, like birth certificates, employment records, a previous address, or even a criminal record. Do me another favor, too. Find out who lives at Forty-Eight Pearl Street in Santa Monica. Yes, I have a telephone book, but I want more than just a name...if it's not too much trouble. Thank you, Barney. Call me as soon as you find something."

He hung up and sat back down in his chair. Well, that just complicated things. It seems Vivian and her sister didn't exist before they arrived in Los Angeles six years ago.

Preston sat there, staring at the photos and going through the stack of notes in his head, when someone tapped softly on the door. He caught a smile and got up to open it. As he expected, his sweet, sixty-year-old mother stood there wearing a full-length floral print dress. "Well, don't you look lovely this afternoon, Mother?"

She gazed up at him with her blue eyes and rosy cheeks. "The Jansens will be here soon. Will you be joining us? They're looking forward to seeing you."

"I'll pop in and say hello, but I have an appointment at one o'clock, and I don't want to be late."

"Preston, you're always so busy these days, we barely see you."

His mother only stood five feet tall, so Preston bent way down and gently kissed the top of her head. "Now, that's not true, Mother. I'll meet you downstairs in a few minutes."

Preston was smiling as he closed the door, but the telephone rang again, and he hurried over to answer it. "What have you got, Barney?" He wrote the information down. "Okay, keep looking. Thanks."

He studied the information. Arthur Romano was fifty-two years old, and he purchased the home on Pearl Street in cash six years ago. That, alone, seemed a little too coincidental. So far, that's all Barney could find out about him.

Preston finally went downstairs and visited with his parents and the Jansens for a few minutes. Then he went outside and hopped into his red Jaguar. He took the side roads to Hollywood Boulevard to avoid the lights, made it to the Bank of America in record time, and parked at the curb out front.

Both he and his father kept all their financial accounts at the Bank of California in San Francisco, so Preston had the perfect excuse to inquire about this bank's facilities as well as their security. And with his family's wealth and notoriety, he was pretty sure they would treat him like royalty.

As he approached the front door, he saw his good friend, Nick Campbell, through the window. He was standing at one of the counters against the wall inside the bank where customers filled out checks and deposit tickets. Preston nodded to him and entered the bank. There were four teller stations along the back wall with a handful of customers in line, and two doors to his right that he assumed were offices for the manager and assistant manager. There was also a security guard standing in the corner on his left.

A middle-aged woman with short, brown hair and thick eyeglasses quickly approached him. "Good afternoon, are you Mister Stone?"

"Yes," he replied.

"I'm Wanda Schwinn, the senior bank teller. Mister Goldman is waiting for you in his office. It's right this way." She led him to the first door and opened it. "Mister Stone is here."

Preston stepped inside the room, and Thomas Goldman, the manager, hurried over to shake his hand. He was a thin man, smartly dressed, and he wore a gold wedding band.

"It's a pleasure to meet you, Mister Stone."

"Thank you for taking time out of your schedule. As I mentioned over the telephone, I have a few rather large accounts that I'm thinking about transferring to your facility. My father and I have been banking in San Francisco for years, but I would prefer having my funds close at hand."

"Yes, of course, I understand," Thomas said with an eagerness in his voice that was almost laughable. "We appreciate your consideration. First, Wanda and I will show you around our facility, which was remodeled three years ago. Then we'll come back to my office and go over the different accounts available, the interest rates and terms, and I'll answer any questions you might have."

Wanda began the tour by introducing him to each of the tellers and giving him a little information about them, which Preston knew was a cunning tactic to personalize his visit. Next, they took him down a hallway to the vaults in the back.

"How long have you worked here, Mister Goldman?" Preston asked.

"Please, call me Thomas. I was hired as a teller five years ago and became assistant manager after two years of intensive training. Last year, I was promoted to the manager's position."

"That's quite impressive." Of course, Preston was doing the math in his head. The man appeared to be around his age, early to mid-thirties, and he wondered what Thomas did before he became a teller. "Did the previous manager retire?"

"No. He...had an unfortunate accident last fall," Thomas stated, earning a scowl from Wanda, which Preston found interesting. Of course, the truth would have sounded rather dubious given the fact that George Ramsey died of a gunshot wound during a robbery right up the street from the bank on Hollywood Boulevard.

Thomas pulled out a ring of keys as they stopped in front of the gate. He opened it and pointed to the mammoth silver vault inside the room while explaining that both this vault and the one beside them on the adjacent wall consisted of a steel-reinforced concrete door that was at least a foot thick and weighed twenty metric tons. They were also protected with complex combination locks and only he, Wanda, and the bank president knew the combination.

After closing the gate, Thomas stepped over to the other vault. He kept his back to them and his actions hidden as he opened it. "This is the safe deposit box room for customers who want to lock up their valuables, such as jewelry, collectibles, heirlooms, legal paperwork, whatever the need. Wanda and I are the only employees who possess a set of keys to each deposit box in case the owner forgets or misplaces theirs."

Preston walked around the spacious room. "Your security is outstanding, and I certainly will need to reserve one of the safe deposit boxes. May I ask what happens in the event a customer forgets their key and neither of you are available?"

"Wanda and I have arranged our work schedules to guarantee one of us is always present at the bank."

"That's commendable of you both. I think I've seen enough. Why don't we head back to your office?" Preston continued chatting with them as Thomas locked up. He began asking them more personal questions about their families, spouses, and pastimes, and he discovered Thomas lived in Chicago before moving to California.

Twenty minutes later, Preston left the bank with a folder of information and Thomas' business card, which he immediately handed to Nick, who was waiting for him on the corner. "Goldman acts like a pretty ordinary guy, but he's hiding something. Find out all you can about Mister Goldman's previous life in Chicago."

"I had a nice little chat with Betty, one of the tellers. She's been working here for over seven years. She heard about Willoughby's death but couldn't remember the last time she saw him. Betty also thinks very highly of Wanda Schwinn, her supervisor. I guess they socialize together after work sometimes."

"She seemed pretty straightforward."

"Yeah but get this. When I asked Betty about Thomas Goldman, she clammed right up and looked madder than a badger caught in a rusty old bear trap. I couldn't get another thing out of her."

Preston glared at him. "Where the hell do you come up with these analogies?"

Nick laughed. "My nephew and I are reading a book about Davy Crockett."

"That explains it," he chuckled. "I'm going to pay the Willoughby's a visit and give them my condolences in person. According to their files, they're one big, happy family, but I can't believe there isn't at least a little friction between the three siblings. Stop by the estate later this afternoon. We need to wrap this up as quickly as possible."

8

Best Friends

It was close to two o'clock by the time Vivian returned to the boutique. She opened the side door, and Bella happily greeted her. Then she noticed Missus Benedetti on the raised platform in the corner of the room with Nora standing beside her. She had forgotten all about the woman's fitting appointment.

Nora saw her and hurried over. "Vivian, I hope you don't mind, but I pulled out your design pattern for Missus Benedetti's gown and started taking her measurements."

"I don't mind at all. I feel terrible for being gone for so long. Thank you for covering for me. Why don't you continue with her measurements? I'll say hello to her and stay close by in case you have any questions, but I'm sure you're doing just fine."

Vivian greeted Missus Benedetti, and after they spoke, she went into the display room to take care of any walk-in customers. It wasn't long before Nora finished with Missus Benedetti, and while she escorted the woman out, Vivian took a pencil and pad with her and disappeared into the storage room off the hallway. She turned on the light and opened the top drawer of the filing cabinet.

After she set several folders that contained receipts and bank records aside, she found the one she was looking for and opened it up. It was a carbon copy of the police report from the night George died. She had requested it from the police department when she realized they had all but given up the search for Elliott Kimball.

Vivian read through the entire report again. This time, she jotted down the names of the two witnesses who had claimed they recognized the gunman as Kimball. She also noted that the gun used to kill George was a Smith and Wesson thirty-eight caliber pistol, which was a favorite among police officers.

Now that she suspected Captain Kynette, she wondered if he or someone else, like the mayor, had paid the witnesses to point the finger at Kimball. Or maybe the witnesses didn't exist at all.

"Excuse me, Vivian," Nora called from the doorway, startling the daylights out of her. "Miss Lombard is here to pick up her order. I thought you'd want to take care of her."

"She is?" So badly, Vivian had wanted to talk to Carole about George. She even drove by Carole's house twice on her way home from Santa Monica earlier, but telling her about George's affair meant explaining *how* she learned about it. "Thank you, Nora. I'll be right out."

Vivian tucked the report back into the folder, but she left the bank records on top of the cabinet. She had always taken care of her business income and expenses, and George took care of their personal accounts. After his death, she never went through those accounts looking for questionable expenses on his part. Now, she intended to go through them with a fine-toothed comb.

Finally, she headed into the display room out front and found Carole looking through the racks of summer dresses along the far wall. "Hello, Carole, I'm glad you're here."

Carole held up a red and white sleeveless polka dot dress she took from the rack. "Vivian, this is absolutely charming!" She held it up to herself. "I love it."

"It should be your size. I'll have Nora wrap it up for you as a gift. Do you have time to go upstairs with me for a few minutes?"

Carole looked at her and put the dress back on the rack. "What's wrong?"

"Oh, there's a whole lot wrong." She roped her arm through Carole's, and they went into the back room. "Nora, we're going upstairs for a bit. Why don't you pull out the roll of material and get the pattern pieces ready for Missus

Benedetti's gown? I won't be long." The two of them went up to her apartment. "Before I tell you anything, Carole, promise me that you won't tell a soul."

"Of course, I promise."

Vivian opened her door, and they went into the kitchen. Carole sat down at the table while she paced across the room. "A woman called me on Monday afternoon and said she had some information and wanted to meet with me. I didn't know what it was about, but when I arrived at her hotel, the door to her room was ajar, so I went inside." She handed the photograph to Carole. "I found that picture of the woman and George on the coffee table."

"That bastard!" Carole swore. "He was cheating on you?"

Vivian stopped her frantic trek and plopped down the chair next to her. "That's not all, Carole. The woman was on the floor, dead. Someone shot her."

"Dead! What the hell did you do?"

"I took the photograph and hightailed it down the back stairway out of the hotel."

Vivian didn't know why she'd left Preston out of her summary of what had happened. He had a whole lot to do with it, maybe even more than she imagined, and it's not like Carole didn't know about her contempt for the man. She also didn't mention Tilly's affair with the mayor or share the conclusions she'd drawn when she was at the docks in Marina del Rey since they were just theories.

"No one saw me go into the hotel or leave," Vivian said. "Her name was Tilly Trimble. According to the news, the police are still investigating her murder."

"Thank goodness no one saw you. Was she going to tell you about their affair? Is that why she called?"

"I assume so."

Carole glanced at the picture again. "Did you know her or ever see her before?"

"No…I wondered if you did. She was a young actress."

"Oh, Viv…" Carole set the picture down and reached over to cup her hand over hers. "I had no idea that George was seeing someone, if that's what you're thinking."

"I'm sorry. I just feel like such a fool. Some of his friends probably knew about it, like David."

"I remember you talking about him. Wasn't he in real estate?"

"Yes, David helped us find the house in Glendale, and George was going to put an offer on it." Vivian pulled her hand away. "Or was that another lie?" She remembered talking to David on the phone only a few hours before George died. When she asked David about the house in Glendale, he said it was available, but he seemed uncomfortable now that she thought about it. His voice had quieted, and he hemmed and hawed and told her to have George call him. "Today is Tuesday, isn't it?"

"Yes, why?"

"It's golf day. At least it used to be for George. He, David, Stu, and Chuck always left work a little early to play eight holes of golf and ended up going to Perino's Restaurant for a few drinks afterward."

"Oh, boy, what do you have up your sleeve?" Carole asked.

"I'm going to sound like a vindictive shrew right now, but I want to go to Perino's and see if they show up. David knew about George's affair, Carole. I'm sure of it now. His wife calls me occasionally, but I haven't seen any of them since George's funeral. If I'm right about David, I want him to know that I found out about the affair. It would make me feel a lot better and not so stupid. Will you go with me?"

Carole's eyes lit up. "You bet your...*behind* I'll go with you. And you're not stupid or vindictive. What George did was rotten to the core, and you deserve to give his friends a piece of your mind if they knew about it. Clark has a business meeting with his press agent, so I'm free as a bird. I'll drive us to Perino's. What time did you want me to pick you up?"

"The boutique closes at six o'clock."

"Perfect." Carole leaned over and hugged her tightly. "Don't worry, Viv. You're going to be just fine."

The first thing Vivian did after Carole left was call Maria, who lived next door. Vivian never left Bella at home by herself, and Tony Martino's wife was a wonderful woman who told her to bring Bella over whenever she needed someone to watch her. With that arranged, Vivian helped Nora with Missus Benedetti's gown the rest of the afternoon.

At six o'clock, she closed the boutique, and Carole arrived in her sporty BMW roadster, wearing the sleeveless polka dot dress she had admired earlier.

Vivian grabbed her handbag, and the second Vivian got into the passenger seat and closed the door, Carole sped off, heading for Wilshire Boulevard.

"The two of us haven't gone out together in over a month," Carole said. "We're going to have a great time, and if we get bored at Perino's or if we end up causing a big scene, we can always leave and finish the night off at the Brown Derby."

"I don't plan on making a scene. I just want to say hello to David if he's there and ask him a few *harmless* questions. Of course, there's always a chance that either guilt or embarrassment might cause him to make a scene."

"Just put him on the spot and put him in his place, Vivian, and our night will be a success."

Perino's was only a five-minute drive. Carole barely slowed down when she pulled into the parking lot and squeezed into a tight spot in the front row. The two of them entered the restaurant, and the maître de hurried over to them.

"Good evening, Miss Lombard! It is good to see you again. Your favorite table is available in the dining room."

"Not tonight, Gabriel. Miss Steele and I would like a table for two in the cocktail lounge, preferably close to the bar."

"Certainly, please follow me." He led them down two steps into the large lounge that held twenty tables, a thirty-foot mahogany bar that stretched across one wall with a large crowd, and a small stage with an older gentleman playing soft background tunes on the piano. Gabriel stopped in front of a table along the adjacent wall. "Is this location suitable?"

"Yes, Gabriel, it's perfect," Carole said. "Thank you."

He set their menus down and pulled the chairs out for them. "Annette will be your cocktail waitress. Please feel free to order anything you wish off the menu. Have a good evening, ladies."

Before Carole took her seat, she waved to someone across the room. "Katherine Hepburn is here! We haven't seen each other in months. I'll stop by her table later and say hello. I see she's with Howard Hughes, the movie producer. He and Katherine have been a hot item for a couple of years now. Any sign of David or his friends?"

Vivian shook her head. "No."

Annette approached their table, and they both ordered a margarita. Carole also asked for an order of crabmeat stuffed celery and shrimp cocktail for two. "I'm starving, and if I know you, Vivian, you haven't eaten all day."

She didn't respond. David, Stu, and Chuck just walked into the lounge and headed straight for the bar. "They're here, George's friends."

"Where?" Carole asked, stretching her neck to see.

At the same time, Vivian turned away from them, thinking about last summer when she and George went to David and Julie's house in Arlington Heights. Stu and Chuck were there, too, with their wives, and they all had such a wonderful time. "Maybe this wasn't such a good idea…"

"Which one is David?"

"The shorter, dark-haired man."

Carole leaned closer and whispered to her. "Okay, here's the plan. Annette is bringing our drinks over now. Take a few good, hearty gulps of your margarita. That'll help you get your nerve back. And if you're still not up to it, you may not even need to talk to him. Catch David's attention and watch his reaction. That might be enough to tell you where he stands. Then you can decide what you want to do about it. If all else fails, I wouldn't mind taking a swing at all three of them for you."

After Annette set their drinks down and left, Vivian stared at her glass and ran her fingertip around the salty rim. "I feel like such an idiot. It never crossed my mind for a minute that George was…"

"Stop that right now!" Carole scolded. "Wallowing in self-pity won't do any good. Believe me, I know. Once we finish this business with George's friends, you need to put it behind you and move on. That's all any of us can do in situations like this."

Vivian looked up at her. Carole was right. Actually, those were the exact words that Arthur would have said to her if she had talked to him earlier. Instead, she sat in front of his house until he peeked out the window.

The trouble was, she had already put so many years of her life behind her, she couldn't let this go. Not until she knew the truth. All of it. Otherwise, she would just keep making the same mistake.

"Viv, didn't you say David was married?" Carole asked. "Is that his wife with him over there?"

She glanced toward the bar. David had his arm wrapped tightly around a beautiful brunette's waist, and he was whispering in her ear. "No, that is definitely not Julie. And those other two women aren't Stu's or Chuck's wives either. So...this is what they did after they went golfing every Tuesday. I think I'll have a few more sips of my drink like you said and go over to the bar to say *hello* to them."

9

Perino's

Vivian sat at the table and watched David and the others for a few more minutes. "Well, here goes nothing."

"Are you sure you don't want me to go with you?" Carole asked.

"No, it's better if I do this by myself."

"Remember what I said. Put those weasels on the spot, put them in their place, and walk away with your head held high."

She flashed a grin at Carole and headed through the crowd. David was leaning against the bar with his back to her now, conversing with the others, and the brunette couldn't have stood any closer to him if she tried.

Vivian rested her elbow on the bar directly behind David, and the bartender immediately rushed over to her. She shook her head. "I'm all set. Thank you."

Chuck noticed her first, and he nudged Stu. Then David glanced over his shoulder and took a double take. Carole was right again. All three of them looked guilty as sin.

She smiled. "Hello, David."

"Vivian! It's...it's good to see you again."

She nodded to Chuck and Stu, and they both mumbled some sort of awkward greeting. "It's been a long time, fellas," she went on. "You're all looking well." Intentionally, she ignored the brunette, who was staring at her with grating curiosity. "I see the three of you are still playing golf on Tuesday. George used to enjoy it so much. It was his *favorite* day of the week."

David cleared his throat. "Yeah, we miss him. At least they finally caught the man responsible."

"I read about it in the newspaper. That's such a relief. Did you hear that Tilly Trimble was murdered yesterday? You knew her, didn't you? What a shame. She was so young. I wonder who killed her? Anyway, I won't take up any more of your time. I just wanted to see how you were all doing. Have a good evening."

She moved to leave, but she wasn't finished yet and turned to face them again. "Oh, I nearly forgot, David. Please give your wife, Julie, my best. I hope your kids are doing well, too. Chuck and Stu, tell your wives that I said hello."

With that, she turned around and made her grand exit back to her table, smiling and holding her head up high. Then she collapsed in her chair. "Did you see their faces?"

"Holy crap, that was priceless!" Carole laughed. "It's not over, either. I don't know what the heck you said to them, but all three women are furious." She took a sip of her drink and nearly spit it back out. "Quick, Vivian, look! The brunette just threw her drink right in David's face, and she's screaming at him. You think I use foul language. Listen to her!"

Vivian snickered. "My, she does have a temper, doesn't she? Even the poor bartender can't calm her down."

"Here comes Gabriel. He'll either settle the girls down or toss them out the door."

The two of them sat there, staring at the heated spectacle, along with most of the other patrons. Finally, the brunette snatched her purse, spouted off at David again, and led the way out of the lounge with the other two women right behind her. To top Vivian's night off, Gabriel spoke to David, Chuck, and Stu and asked them to leave the premises.

"Show's over," Carole laughed. "Well done, Viv."

"That felt wonderful." She picked up a piece of stuffed celery and sat back in her seat, munching on it.

"Crap, you'll never guess who just showed up to spoil your moment of glory."

Vivian looked behind her. Preston Stone stood in the doorway with one of his platinum-blonde trophies clutching his arm, a young woman who barely looked old enough to drink and wore a revealing flamingo-pink gown. Preston grinned like a Cheshire cat as he gathered everyone's attention. Then he threw his hand into the air, waved to the crowd, and headed for the bar.

Vivian hoped for his sake he kept his distance from her tonight. She wasn't in the mood to lock horns with him again, especially after what they went through at the hotel yesterday.

"I know Preston is a rascal," Carole said as she watched him. "I also understand your resentment toward him for hurting Patricia, but she's happier than a lark now, isn't she? You said she's marrying a terrific guy in a few months."

"Yes...but look at him. Preston is so pompous and full of himself. The only difference between him and George and his golfing buddies is that he's not married. That still doesn't give him the right to use women for his own amusement and then dump them the minute he grows tired of them."

"There is another difference between Preston and the others," Carole told her. "With Preston, what you see is what you get. He has never put on pretenses of being anything other than what he is, a flamboyant and incorrigible playboy. Patricia knew all about him when she started seeing him."

Vivian couldn't argue that point. She had even warned Patricia about Preston herself, but her sister refused to listen and went out with him, anyway. Then she cried on her shoulder for a month before deciding to move back to New York City. "Why are you suddenly defending him, Carole?"

"I don't think I want to tell you now. You'll get mad at me."

"Don't be silly."

Carole hesitated. "Preston and his parents are coming to my garden party on Thursday. I had to invite them. Randolph and Nita Stone are very nice people and generous to a fault. They've donated to so many worthy causes. I don't want you to change your mind about coming to it just because Preston will be there."

"I expected him to come," she told Carole. "He's invited to every function in California."

"Well, then hopefully you won't mind that I also took the liberty of sending an invitation to Gary Rutherford."

Vivian couldn't believe her ears. "You did what?"

"Don't look so surprised. You know how meddlesome I can be, especially when it comes to affairs of the heart. I saw you talking with him at your fashion show last Friday. You said you were hoping to hear from him."

"I meant for business reasons, not personal!"

"Well, I thought you'd enjoy seeing him again. Don't worry. I cleverly invited several other executives from Bullock's, so it wouldn't seem so obvious. You need to look to the future, Viv. You're too young to spend it alone. After what you discovered tonight, I think it's perfect timing, and you should thank me."

Annette approached their table, silencing Vivian. "Ladies, these cocktails are from the gentleman at the bar." She set two more margaritas on the table.

Carole smiled at Vivian. "See? Preston Stone isn't such a bad rogue after all."

"They aren't from Mister Stone," Annette said.

"Who bought them?" Vivian asked.

"Mister Shaw, the mayor's brother. He's standing at the other end of the bar."

They both looked over, but Vivian was the only one who caught a frown as Joe Shaw lifted his drink to them in a toast.

Carole returned his gesture. "Well, this is a surprise. I heard the mayor and his brother were a couple of cheapskates. Thank you, Annette."

Vivian remained silent. She was thinking about the note Captain Kynette had written in the courtroom, and the mayor's brother glancing in her direction after reading it. At the time, she didn't think too much about it, but she certainly did now.

"Okay, where were we?" Carole asked. "Ah, yes, Gary Rutherford. Wipe that scowl off your face. I'm your best friend, and I watch out for you. He's good-looking and successful, and I noticed he wasn't wearing a wedding band. Besides that, the two of you have a lot in common. For heaven's sake, his business is finding the best fashion designers, and you fit into that category ten times over."

"It's too soon for me to think about the future, but I adore you for going to all that trouble. I didn't tell you that Gary Rutherford called this morning and asked to meet me for lunch tomorrow. He's going to show my portfolio to the executives at Bullock's. I'm hoping they decide to carry a line of my designs in their store."

Carole clapped her hands. "Really? That's fantastic."

"I'm keeping my fingers crossed."

"You don't need luck, Vivian. You've got all the talent in the world. That's what it takes."

As the two of them continued talking, Vivian kept shifting uncomfortably in her seat. Out of the corner of her eye, she not only noticed Joe Shaw kept looking over at them as though wanting to catch her attention, but Preston frequently glanced her way. She assumed he was champing at the bit to wander over and spoil the rest of her evening.

To make matters worse, Carole suddenly stood up. "I'll be right back. I want to chat with Katherine and Howard before they leave." And Carole was gone before she could respond.

Vivian didn't want to sit there by herself, so she got up and walked up the steps and down the hall to the restroom. After she reapplied her lipstick and brushed her hair, she waited a few more minutes, pacing back and forth in the small space until another woman entered the restroom.

She headed back to the lounge, hoping Carole had returned to their table. Halfway down the hall, Joe Shaw rounded the corner and walked toward her. There was no turning back, so she quickened her pace, opened her purse, and pretended to be looking for something.

"Good evening," he said. "Miss Steele, isn't it?"

She forced a smile and kept walking, but he deliberately stepped in front of her to block her way.

"I heard the police finally found and killed the man who murdered your husband," Joe told her. "That must have been a great relief to you. I hope you're sleeping better at night."

With that comment, she lifted her steel-gray eyes and glared at the sinister smirk on his pudgy face.

"Vivian, there you are!" Preston called out from down the hall, and he rushed over to them. "Carole has been looking everywhere for you." He nodded to Joe. "How are you doing tonight? Let's go, Vivian. Carole has something to show you." Preston gently took her arm and escorted her to the cocktail lounge, but he stopped at the doorway. "I don't like that man any more than you do. Carole is back at your table. Have a good evening, Vivian."

She couldn't hide her puzzlement as she watched him walk away, but she quickly joined Carole while trying to make sense of what just happened. One thing was for sure, she wanted to leave. The moment they finished their drinks, she feigned being tired and told Carole that she needed to go home to pick up Bella from the neighbors. Carole was sorely disappointed and argued with her about the early hour, but they finally paid the bill and left the restaurant.

After Carole dropped her off, Vivian chatted with Maria for a while. Then she and Bella headed across the alley to their building, but Bella wandered away to do her business in the small grassy yard at the end of the alley. While Vivian waited, she noticed the man across the street, leaning against the Post Office on the corner, smoking a cigarette and looking around, seemingly minding his own business.

She'd seen him standing there a few nights this past week and usually, he had a large canine companion with him. She assumed he lived in the neighborhood, but he always stood by the post office rather than in front of a nearby apartment building.

Bella returned, and they went inside. On the way upstairs, Vivian collected the folders of hers and George's bank records, which she'd left on the filing cabinet in the storage room. Before she turned on the lights in her apartment, she made her way over to the living room window and peeked out.

The man was still in front of the post office.

She quickly closed the curtain, turned on the light, and sat next to Bella on the couch. Carefully, she skimmed through the bank accounts, every expense and deposit. Nearly an hour later, she closed the last folder. There was nothing out of the ordinary that she could find, which seemed odd if George was spending time with Tilly Trimble. The only explanation was that he'd paid cash for any gifts and trips he'd taken with her, but where did the cash come from?

Vivian turned the lights off, and she and Bella went into the bedroom. Bella jumped on the bed while Vivian changed into her satin pajamas and sat at her vanity to brush her hair. The events of the night kept running through her head, everything from seeing David and the others with their girlfriends to Joe Shaw sending her and Carole a drink and cornering her in the hallway.

And for the life of her, she couldn't figure out why Preston had come to her rescue.

10

Opportunities

Wednesday, May 4

Vivian got up early the next morning and went downstairs. She made a pot of coffee and started stacking all the boxes of clothing, accessories, and shoes by the side door to take to the public market.

Every other Wednesday, she closed the boutique for the day. The depression was winding down, but even so, there were many families out of work who had very little money to spend on food and clothing for themselves and their children. For several years, over sixty vendors displayed their wares at the public market, selling fresh produce, meats, seafood, and baked goods at less than half the cost or even pennies on the dollar.

Two years ago, a few clothing and household vendors got together and rented space so they could offer their discounted goods. Ever since, more and more vendors have joined in, and Vivian was proud to be a part of the endeavor.

Nora arrived at eight o'clock, and the two of them loaded the boxes into Vivian's car. When they finished, they sat at the table in the back room of the shop, enjoying a cup of coffee.

"At eleven-thirty, I need to meet Gary Rutherford for lunch, and I'm tossed about going to that premiere later this afternoon. I'm not really in the mood to watch a movie today, but I probably should at least show up at the theater for a bit." Vivian looked down at Bella playing with one of her stuffed toys and smiled. "I'll set Bella up with her bed and toys at our booth. She enjoys going to the market and playing with the children. Maria said she would watch her from across the aisle, but could you make sure Tony doesn't feed Bella too many treats? It's so sweet of him, but the last time, he fed her too much, and she and I both paid for it later."

Nora laughed. "I'll take care of it."

When it was time to leave, Vivian grabbed her handbag and portfolio, and they got into the car. She drove to the Grand Central Market on South Broadway, and as always, the city traffic was extremely heavy, coming to a near standstill less than half a mile away from the market.

Nora glanced around. "There's Clifton's Brookdale Cafeteria. My friends and I love eating there. The décor is so unique. It's like walking into a national park with tall columns made from redwood trees, and rocks and foliage decorating the walls. There's also a stream running right through the dining room. It's amazing, and their food is wonderful. Have you ever been there?"

"No, but that's where I'm meeting Gary Rutherford for lunch. I've seen pictures of the interior, and I keep meaning to stop by there sometime. I also heard about their *'pay what you wish'* policy for those who can't afford a hot meal. The owners sound like very generous people."

"Clinton and Neda Clifford care a lot about the community. Remember yesterday when we were talking about the Kynette trial and all the rumors about the mayor's illegal activities? Well, Mister Clifford is the chairman of CIVIC, a group of citizens lobbying against the political corruption in the city, specifically against the mayor. They've been gathering information to take to the grand jury, hoping to remove him from office."

"I've never heard of them. I'm impressed, Nora. You're very knowledgeable about our local politics."

She laughed. "I have a few friends who go to the political extreme. You have to kind of sift through the things they say and choose what to believe. When I think they have a good point, I research it a little more, and they were right about Mister Clifford's efforts. He's gained a lot of support from the public, but he's also gotten plenty of flak from city officials."

"I can imagine."

Traffic started moving again, and Vivian parked right in front of the market temporarily to unload the boxes and carry them to their rented space inside. When they finished, Nora started unpacking while Vivian moved her car to the lot behind the building. The two of them quickly set up the displays with separate racks for house dresses, afternoon dresses, and evening wear. Hats, scarves, gloves, handbags, and lingerie were meticulously arranged on portable shelves, along with the few dozen pairs of shoes donated from the shoe store across the street.

Wednesdays were always one of the busiest days at the Grand Central Market, and today was no exception. At eleven fifteen, Vivian made sure Nora and Bella were all set, and she walked to Brookdale's Cafeteria down the road. She entered the multi-level restaurant, and she was stunned by the rustic, park-like scenery and décor.

The hostess immediately greeted her. Vivian mentioned she was meeting Gary Rutherford, and the woman said he was waiting for her on the lower level. They walked down the stairs and followed the small creek that ran through the center of the dining room.

Gary was sitting at one of the tables. He saw her and stood up. "It's good to see you again, Vivian. Have a seat."

"I can't thank you enough for this opportunity. I brought my portfolio with me." She handed it to him, smiling sweetly, although silently, she was cursing Carole.

If her good friend hadn't gone on about Gary's credentials as a potential suitor last night, she wouldn't be focusing on his appearance right now. As it was, she noticed he was quite handsome and well-dressed in a three-piece brown herringbone suit. He stood nearly six feet tall, with hazel eyes and dark hair that was as neatly groomed as his attire.

For the next hour, Vivian thoroughly enjoyed both their lunch and their conversation. After they ordered sandwiches, they went through her portfolio together. Again, Gary seemed extremely impressed. He explained the executives were looking for fresh and unique designs to carry at their Wilshire Branch, and he felt hers would be perfect. From there, the topic steered away from business, and she found Gary delightful to talk with. So much so, she was almost disappointed when he paid the check, and they got up to leave.

"I'm going to present your portfolio to the executives at our meeting first thing Friday morning," he told her as they walked to the front door. "I should have their answer within a day or two."

"Thank you for taking the time to meet with me. I saw Carole Lombard last night. She's a good friend of mine. I think she sent an invitation to you for the charity event at her home tomorrow afternoon. It's such a worthy cause. Will you be going?"

"Why yes, I'm looking forward to it." He opened the front door for her. "Can I give you a lift back to the public market?"

Vivian didn't answer right away. As soon as she stepped outside, she saw Lucky standing directly across the street from her. He was waiting at the bus stop and had spotted her, too. She didn't want to acknowledge him since their association needed to remain a secret, but it was the expression on Lucky's face that held her attention a few seconds longer.

When Gary repeated the question, she turned to him. "No, it's just a short walk to the market. Thank you again. I will see you at Carole's tomorrow."

Vivian headed down the sidewalk, excited about how well her meeting went with Gary. Then she remembered what Nora had told her earlier about the owner of Brookdale Cafeteria, and seeing Lucky had spurred her curiosity. There was no doubt in her mind that the mayor and his brother were involved not only in George's death but Tilly Trimble's as well. She wanted to hear more about the group called CIVIC and hoped the owner might be willing to talk with her about it.

With that decided, she made sure Gary was out of sight, turned around, and went back inside the restaurant. She asked the hostess if Mister Clifford was available, and the woman pointed to the table in the corner on the first level.

Vivian walked over to him. "Excuse me, Mister Clifford? My name is Vivian Steele. I wondered if I could speak with you for a moment?"

He stood up and kindly pulled the chair out for her. "Of course, have a seat. Can I get you something to drink?"

"No, I'm fine. I've never been to your restaurant before, and I regret it now. The entire place is simply breathtaking, and the food was delicious."

"Thank you. My wife and I wanted to create an atmosphere that was as relaxing and comfortable as...well, as walking through a park."

"You certainly accomplished that. I won't take up much of your time. A friend of mine mentioned your involvement in a group called CIVIC. I wondered if I could ask you a few questions about it?"

He hesitated. "That depends on your purpose, Miss Steele. If you heard about our group, then you probably realize that we've made plenty of friends as well as enemies. I've learned the hard way that I need to tread lightly when speaking with others about it."

"I assure you that my reasons are strictly personal and not political. I own a small fashion boutique in Beverly Hills, and frankly, I was going to ask you to keep our conversation between us."

With a genuine smile, he took his spectacles off and placed them on the table. "What did you want to know?"

"I wondered if it's true that your organization is hoping to remove the mayor from office?"

He nodded. "Yes, along with a few of his closest political cronies. We've had quite a struggle. Not only is the grand jury very specific about the evidence we need to provide to accomplish our goal, but those opposing our efforts have blatantly attacked some of our members, including myself. Last summer I was elected chairman of CIVIC, and I took an oath to root out public corruption in the city no matter the source. In doing so, I immediately faced phony sanitation violations here at the cafeteria. My new permits were denied, stink bombs were left in kitchens and bathrooms, and food poisoning complaints poured in. I could go on."

His speech silenced her for a few minutes. "All that didn't stop you from pursuing it?"

"I've learned nothing worthwhile comes easy. Of course, I'm far less verbal about our group's intentions now and even more determined to end the mayor's reign over the city." He studied her for a moment, then he leaned back and folded his hands in his lap. "Why don't you tell me why you're inquiring about this?"

She looked at him directly. "I was in the courtroom earlier to watch Captain Kynette's trial. I strongly believe he killed my husband last fall at a drugstore on Hollywood Boulevard, upon the mayor's orders."

"What was your husband's name?"

"George Ramsey."

He shook his head. "I'm not familiar with his case, but it's possible. During the past few years, Captain Kynette has committed multiple criminal acts. Is your husband's death included as one of the charges against him?"

"No, I think the police falsified witness records to place the blame on another known criminal. That man was killed in a stakeout last Saturday night, and my husband's case was closed. I was hoping you might have heard about George's death or run across information about it."

He reached over and placed his hand over hers. "I'm sorry about your husband. You may not want to hear this, but you need to put it behind you and stay out of this fight. Let us finish what we started. Despite the mayor's aggressive actions, we're compiling strong solid evidence against him and the others. We just need another month to present our findings to the grand jury."

"So, you don't have any advice or suggestions on how I could find out if Captain Kynette was behind my husband's death? The owner of the drugstore was also killed that same night."

"You're not listening to me, Miss Steele," he stated firmly. "These men, the mayor, his brother, and even James Davis, the chief of police, will stop at nothing to achieve their own gain. Please do not go off on your own trying to find out the truth. Believe me, if they even have an inkling that you've been looking into their illegal activities, they will retaliate against you without blinking an eye. Then they will shove it under the rug as they have done to so many others. I'll tell you what. You and I will keep in touch, discreetly, and I will let you know when we meet with the grand jury."

As much as she wanted to argue with him, she fell silent. She had no intention of letting this go. He seemed very determined, and she supposed he would reach his goal eventually, but simply removing the mayor and his associates from office wasn't enough. They needed to be held accountable for possibly three deaths on top of it.

11

'A Pocketful of Coins'

Vivian returned to the public market. She was disappointed that Mister Clifford was no help at all, but she was on cloud nine after her enjoyable meeting with Gary Rutherford. Nora couldn't wait to hear all about her luncheon, and then the two of them worked together for the next hour and a half until Vivian grudgingly had to leave again.

After she left the market, she drove to Sunset Boulevard. She wasn't sure where the Liberty Theater was located, so she slowed down and scanned the area at each intersection. She continued driving east and worried she'd passed by it, but after a quarter of a mile, she noticed the fancy theater sign on the brick building at the next corner. There was street parking only. Luckily, she found an open spot in front of the newsstand beside the theater.

Vivian checked her wristwatch and noticed she was five minutes early, which was perfect timing, not the first person to arrive and not the last. She made her way to the front entrance of the theater and opened the door.

The first thing she saw was the poster propped up on a tripod stating that the premiere was for the new movie titled *'A Pocketful of Coins'*, starring Nan Grey and Robert Wilcox. Vivian had never heard of the movie, but Nan Grey was one of her new clients and a film actress, so she realized Nan must have sent the invitation to her.

The next thing she noticed was the quaint yet dingy lobby that was no more than twenty feet long, and there wasn't a soul in sight. From the look of things, she concluded that this was the initial private preview of the movie rather than the public premiere, which seemed odd, but she supposed she should feel honored for being invited.

Vivian walked over, pulled the auditorium door open, and stopped in the doorway. There was only one person in the audience sitting in the center seat about midway down. Instantly, an icy chill ran through her. "What's going on, Preston?" she called out.

He turned around and looked just as surprised to see her. "I have no idea."

The ceiling lights suddenly dimmed, and the film projector high above her head started humming and whirring with a steady clicking sound as the large screen against the far wall lit up.

Vivian didn't know if confusion, anger, curiosity, or fear held her there, possibly all of them, but she didn't move from the doorway as she stared wide-eyed at the white screen with the big black numbers slowly counting down from twenty. It was almost hypnotizing until the title appeared.

Then, the black and white movie, void of sound and obviously of poor quality, began.

For the next seven minutes, neither Vivian nor Preston moved a muscle as they watched the film. The first scene showed a blonde woman wearing a blazer and skirt opening a door in what looked to be an apartment building. A dark-haired man stood there dressed in a casual summer suit with a paisley neck scarf tucked into his shirt collar. The two of them smiled at one another, and the woman motioned for him to come inside.

After the man sat down on the couch, she laughed at something he said and stuck her index finger in the air, letting him know that she would return shortly. As soon as the woman left the room, the man lost his smile and quickly started searching the room. He rummaged through the desk drawers, pulled out books on the shelf to look behind them, and combed through the coat closet by the entryway.

The woman walked back into the room carrying two cocktails. She saw what he was doing and panicked. She dropped the drinks on the floor and

A PERILOUS PREMIERE 67

hurried over to grab her purse from the end table. The man darted forward and caught her by the waist. Furiously, the two of them struggled for the handbag. He shoved her back against the wall, and the purse flew into the air.

The next scene focused on the small pouch that fell out of the purse. As it dropped to the ground, twenty or thirty coins spilled out of it and rolled across the floor.

The two actors stared at the coins while the camera moved to the front door. It slowly opened, and a third person, a faceless man, stood in the doorway. He pulled a gun out of his jacket pocket, pointed it at the man, and pulled the trigger. The man jerked backward and fell to the floor. The woman screamed in horror, although no sound came from her. Panic-stricken, she turned around to run away, but the faceless man shot her in the back.

The last scene showed the two of them lying dead on the floor with the coins scattered all around them. Then the camera zoomed in on the woman's blazer and the fancy emblem of Vivian's boutique embroidered on the front pocket. Next, it moved to the man's neck scarf with Preston's initials.

The scene faded out by focusing on the killer's shoes as he reached down to pick up each of the coins, and the words, *The End*, appeared on the screen.

Vivian backed away into the lobby.

Preston charged up the aisle and brushed past her. "Go outside, Vivian!" he shouted as he ran to the door at the end of the lobby and darted up the stairs.

She rushed out the front door and ran to her car, but she sat there, gripping the steering wheel so tightly her knuckles turned white while her heart pounded in her ears.

Preston suddenly burst out the front door of the theater. He saw her sitting there and shouted to her. Frantically, she searched for her purse, grabbed her car keys, and stuck the key into the ignition.

"Vivian, wait!" Preston yelled.

She shoved the shifter into first gear and sped down the road. Skillfully, she weaved her way through traffic at an excessive speed while the movie kept replaying over and over again in her mind.

As soon as she arrived at the market, she parked out front. She instructed Nora to pack up their merchandise even though they usually stayed another two hours. Nora did as she was told without saying a word and followed Vivian's lead by tossing everything that hadn't been sold back into the empty boxes. Even during their drive to the boutique, Nora remained as quiet as a mouse, and Vivian imagined her dear friend was too afraid to speak.

After they finished unloading the car and the boxes were piled in the back room, Nora stood there, biting her bottom lip nervously. "Did I do something wrong, Vivian?"

She went over to hug her. "No, of course not. I...I heard some bad news after I left the theater. That's what upset me." She forced a smile and cupped her cheeks. "We'll talk about it in the morning, okay?"

"Whatever it is, I'm here for you."

"I know. Thank you, Nora. Don't worry. I'll be fine."

As soon as Nora left, she marched over to the garment rack, which was crammed with blouses, skirts, slacks, and housedresses. Her red blazer wasn't on the first clothes hanger, where she always hung it, and like a maniac, she rifled through the entire rack. Her jacket with the boutique emblem embroidered on the breast pocket was missing.

Bella sat there staring at her with her ears back. Vivian felt terrible for scaring both her and Nora. After they went upstairs to the apartment, Vivian closed the door and leaned against it, taking a few deep breaths. She'd been in panic situations before, and the first thing she needed to do was calm down so she could make sense of what happened, and what she saw.

As her heartbeat slowed, she pushed herself away from the door and went into the kitchen to pour herself a glass of red wine. She took a few sips and a few more deep breaths.

At the theater, she had jumped to the conclusion that Preston had concocted the whole thing since he was the only other person present in the auditorium. Now that she was thinking more clearly, she remembered the expression on his face when she walked into the auditorium. He genuinely appeared surprised to see her there. He was also depicted in the movie as a victim. She didn't miss the initials on the man's scarf as he lay on the floor, and after the movie ended, Preston certainly reacted as though the contents had shocked him as much as it did her.

But that merely complicated everything even more. If someone else was behind it, then why were she and Preston singled out and targeted? The only connection between them was her sister, who lived three thousand miles away. Of course, that led her directly back to the hotel room when, oddly enough, she and Preston had both arrived at the same time to discover Tilly Trimble murdered.

Her thoughts spun around to her conversation with Mister Clifford earlier, along with his warning. She couldn't believe that the mayor or his brother would construct such an elaborate scheme simply to pass along a warning. From what she'd heard, they were more prone to outright violence.

With her thoughts spinning around, Vivian refilled her glass of wine and went into the living room. She grabbed her drawing pad and a box of charcoal pencils from her desk and sat down on the couch beside Bella. Putting all else aside, she decided to sketch individual scenes from the movie, hoping it might help her to piece this wicked puzzle together.

She began by sketching a drawing of the woman in the movie as she opened the front door, including the background. Another depicted the woman returning to the room with the cocktails. Then she sketched a couple of pictures of the man wearing the neck scarf, and a separate drawing of the faceless man at the door.

For some reason, the coins held the greatest significance, so she flipped to the next page of her pad and began sketching a few scenes from the end of the movie with the pouch and coins sprinkled across the floor, as well as the third man's two-toned wingtip shoes.

The telephone rang in the kitchen, but she ignored it. It rang again, stopped, and rang a third time. Grumbling under her breath, she walked into the kitchen to answer it. "Hello?" She slammed the receiver down.

It was Preston Stone. Until she made some sort of sense out of this, she didn't want to talk to him or anyone else. When it rang again, she waited until it stopped. Then she set the receiver on the counter, off the hook. After a few minutes of annoying beeping, there was dead silence.

12

Willoughby

Preston poured himself a glass of bourbon from the stocked liquor cart on the pool patio and sat at one of the tables. He was so mad he wanted to put his fist through a wall. As soon as he got home, he searched the dresser and closet in his bedroom for his paisley neck scarf with his initials, but he couldn't find it anywhere. There were two possibilities. He'd either taken it off and left it somewhere, or someone stole it from his room, but the latter seemed pretty remote given the amount of security his father had installed at the estate.

He also made a few phone calls to find out who had access to the theater today. Lo-and-behold, a man claiming to be *him* had called the manager on Monday and offered him a sizeable amount of money to rent the theater for a few hours. The manager readily agreed and received full payment in cash by messenger.

There was no doubt in Preston's mind that he had a very sophisticated nemesis on his hands. Someone who shouldn't be taken lightly or underestimated. Normally, he enjoyed sparring with a formidable opponent since he loved a challenge, but he'd never run across someone so deranged that they would go to all the trouble of making a movie to get their point across.

But what was the point? The movie was meant as a threat to both him and Vivian, but did his adversary know for sure that she had the coins in her possession, or was he merely using her as a decoy to throw him off? Judging from Vivian's reaction at the theater, it could go either way. It was hard to tell whether she was shocked by the contents of the movie or outraged that someone knew she had the coins.

Gunther stepped outside. "Mister Frederick Barcroft is here again, sir."

"You don't have to announce him every time he stops by, Gunther. Just send him out here."

"Yes, sir, but…this time, he has a rather large companion with him named *Boris*."

Preston let out a chuckle. "It's okay. I'll keep an eye on both of them."

Not more than a minute later, he heard Freddie making himself a drink at the liquor cart. Then Boris waltzed by him. He headed straight for the pool, climbed down a couple of steps, and sat in the water as though he owned the joint.

"Hey, Preston," Freddie greeted as he joined him at the table. "What the heck is so urgent? Boris and I didn't even have a chance to finish our dinner."

"Someone else found out the coin collection was missing, and they're trying to get their hands on it before we do."

Freddie lost his smile. "You're kidding? We went to a whole lot of trouble to make sure that information didn't leak out. Willoughby's attorney is the only other person who knows about it besides us."

"Not anymore." Preston took the theater ticket out of his jacket pocket, set it on the table, and slid it over to Freddie. "I received an invitation to a movie premiere the other day. I don't know who sent it. Out of sheer curiosity, I went to the theater this afternoon."

Freddie studied it. "And…"

"You can imagine my surprise when I discovered Vivian Steele was the only other person attending the movie."

"You said she'd be at the public market all day. That's why I didn't follow her."

"I was wrong." He sipped his brandy. "The movie ended up being a crude yet rather absorbing film with a very graphic warning. In a nutshell, the person behind it knows I'm looking for the coins, and he's planning on killing me if I don't give up my efforts. At least that was my take on it."

"Did Steele set you up?"

"On the contrary, the warning was twofold. The mastermind behind the film was letting her know that he intended to kill her if she didn't hand the coins over to him." Preston slid back in his seat and folded his hands in his lap. "Either that, or she doesn't have the coins, and he's trying to steer me in the wrong direction."

"Her husband is one of the six suspects who had access to Willoughby's safe deposit box. He could have taken the coins before he died last fall and either gave them to his wife, or she found them among his belongings afterward. Maybe she's trying to throw you off her scent. We don't know when Willoughby last saw the coins at the bank, do we?"

"No. Nick tried to find out, but we didn't want to be too obvious. The whole purpose of keeping this quiet was to avoid pushing the thief into cashing out the coins. Nick and I have been looking into all the possible suspects, and the people closest to them, but I assumed the coins were stolen within the past two months when Willoughby's health took a turn for the worse. That made the most sense until now. George Ramsey just moved up to the top of the..." Preston suddenly gulped the rest of his drink and got up to pour himself another one.

He stared at the bottle of brandy on the liquor cart. It just occurred to him that George had the perfect motive. In his last love letter to Tilly Trimble, he mentioned wanting to run away together. With two million dollars worth of coins in his pocket, the two of them could have disappeared and lived a grand life anywhere in the world.

"What is it, Preston?"

"I was just thinking that according to the bank records in everyone's files, no one had cashed the coins in."

Freddie chuckled, and a lock of brown hair spilled to his forehead. "You should know better than anyone that whoever took them could have opened an account overseas without anyone finding out. Where does your father keep all his loot?"

"In a bank in San Francisco, Freddie. That's a good point, but judging from the contents of the movie today, I'd have to say the coins are still in the area."

"Getting back to this *mastermind* of the film, how the hell could he know that you were looking for the coins?" Freddie asked.

Preston hesitated to tell him what he thought. Freddie was new at this, although he'd tell you otherwise. He was inexperienced and overly defensive about it. "I have a few thoughts on that, but it's water under the bridge. I'm going to keep track of Vivian from now on. We have a bit of history together, anyway."

"Wait a minute, Preston. You think it's my fault?"

"Like I said, I have a few ideas about it. He might have spotted you trailing Vivian, and one thing led to another."

"That's impossible!" Freddie shouted as he jumped to his feet. "I've been extremely careful. You're always blaming me when things go wrong."

Preston casually glanced over at Boris, who was lying on the pool steps now, completely submerged in the water except for his giant-size head. "Your companion tends to stick out like a sore thumb, Freddie."

"What are you talking about? He's perfect for this line of work! No one would ever suspect what I do for a living when they see him standing next to me. He's big and burly and cute, and he looks harmless, but he's stronger than an ox and tough as nails. I pity anyone who gets on his bad side."

Preston chuckled. "Don't get your feathers in a bunch, as my mother would say. We'll work around it. I have something else I need you to do for me."

Freddie sat down in a huff. "What?"

"Vivian has an assistant at her boutique, a young woman about your age. She's quite attractive, a little unconventional, maybe, but that's right up your alley. Her name is Nora Griswald. She takes a bus to and from the boutique every day except Sunday. Here, I wrote the information down for you."

"You want me to follow her?"

"Feel free to strike up a conversation with her, if you want, but do it discreetly, please. I doubt she knows anything about Vivian's personal business, but until I find out who we're dealing with, the young woman's job at the boutique might put her at risk, too."

Freddie tucked the paper into his pocket. "What about the mayor? Are we putting him on hold?"

"Nick is splitting his time between both projects, but you and I are going to focus on the coins right now."

Freddie finished his drink and looked over at Boris. "I need a couple of towels again."

"There's some in the bathhouse over there," Preston told him. "I'll give you a hand and walk out with you. I have to drop something off to Barney in the city."

"What is it?"

"I took the reel of film before leaving the theater. I'm hoping Barney can give us some idea about who made the movie, along with identifying the actors who starred in it."

"I can take it to him on my way back to my motel," Freddie offered.

"Thanks, but I have a couple of things to discuss with him, anyway."

After they dragged Boris out of the pool and dried him off the best they could, Preston grabbed the briefcase with the film and walked Freddie to his pickup truck out front. Then he found the keys to his father's black Cadillac LaSalle coupe hanging on the wall in the carport and drove that car instead of his Jaguar, so he'd blend in better with the city traffic.

Preston took a roundabout route driving to Alameda Street in downtown Los Angeles, just as a precaution. Along the way, he thought about the six files sitting on his desk in the study, one for each of the original suspects. Three employees at Bank of America had access to Chester Willoughby's safe deposit box: George Ramsey, the previous bank manager; Thomas Goldman, the new manager; and Wanda Schwinn, a senior bank teller.

Chester also had three grown children...heirs to his fortune, two sons and a daughter. All three of them had access to the coins indirectly, and it was possible one of them grew impatient and took the collection before their father's death. For now, the attorney was going to hold off reading Chester's will, hoping they could identify the thief and find the coins.

With two million dollars at stake, all six of them had the means, opportunity, and motive. After reading George's last love letter, he had the greatest financial motive of all, but the crucial question remained...when were the coins stolen, recently or over six months ago? The only way to find out the last time Chester Willoughby had requested access to his safe deposit box and saw the coins for himself was to ask Wanda Schwinn or Thomas Goldman, so he had to figure out a way to do that without alerting them or anyone else.

He thought about Freddie and felt bad assigning the young man the simple task of keeping an eye on Nora Griswald. Preston was sure the two of them would get along, but his sole purpose was to protect both of them. After watching that movie today, things were getting ugly now, and knowing Freddie, he would risk anything, even his life, trying to prove himself. So, it was safer to put a little distance between him and the situation.

Barney was waiting for him on the corner. He and Barney have known each other for several years now, and Preston got a real kick out of him. Barney was a short, stocky fella in his late forties, who complained about everything, had a heart of gold, and his IQ was through the roof, which made him invaluable.

After Preston pulled up to the curb, Barney rested his arms on the open passenger side window. "What have you got for me, Preston?"

He handed Barney the briefcase. "It's a reel of film, just a short clip. I need you to look it over closely and see if you can find out who filmed it, the people who starred in it, where it took place, anything and everything. You'll know why when you watch the film."

"Okay, I'll see what I can do. Did you hear the news? Two of the five felony charges against Captain Kynette were dropped this afternoon, and the prosecutor is up in arms over it. He thinks it's just one step away from Kynette getting off scot-free."

"I guess that isn't surprising, given the mayor's power and connections. I think his brother was out celebrating their victory last night. Does Nick know about it? He's handling the mayor's situation for now."

"He's the one who told me."

"Okay, good. Can you take a look at the film tonight?"

"Sure, why not?" Barney grumbled. "I've been working so many hours my wife isn't speaking to me anymore."

"Don't worry. I'll give Louisa a call, and smooth things over with her. The two of you have your twenty-fifth anniversary coming up soon, don't you? Why don't I arrange for you to spend a week at my father's summer house on Catalina Island? That should make up for all your overtime." Preston thanked him and drove north through the city.

He pulled down Foothill Road and parked near the corner of Third Street, in the shadows of the post office across from Vivian's boutique. It was after eight-thirty now and getting dark, but he could see her car parked in the alley next to her building, and the light was on upstairs.

He'd called her a few times earlier until she took the telephone receiver off the hook. He wasn't even sure what he would have said to her had she answered. His actions were more out of the heat of the moment than anything else.

Preston glanced in his rearview mirror and noticed car headlights slowly creeping up the side road behind him. He waited a minute, and when it got closer, he saw the single red beacon light mounted on the roof of the car. Quickly, he ducked down out of sight, which wasn't easy with his height at six foot two.

After the patrol car crawled by him, he peeked above the dashboard. The car stopped at the corner, then turned left and parked at the curb, directly across from the boutique. Preston scowled as he sat up and stared at the tail end of the car.

He was thinking about last night when Joe Shaw had deliberately cornered Vivian in the hallway at the restaurant. That thought triggered another. He remembered Freddie telling him that Vivian had gone to the courthouse yesterday morning to watch the Kynette trial.

He realized then that there was a hell of a lot more going on in Vivian's life than just dealing with her husband's infidelity and possibly harboring a stolen coin collection.

13

Arthur

Thursday, May 5

The next morning, Vivian went downstairs and put her purse and blue carry bag containing her sketches on the table in the back room of the boutique. Nora would arrive any minute, so she unlocked the front door and tidied up a few things in the display room. Then she sat at the table, waiting.

When Nora arrived, Vivian apologized for her abrupt behavior yesterday and reassured her that everything was fine. "I need to take care of something this morning, and I'll be gone for a few hours."

"Is there anything I can do for you?" Nora asked.

"Just watch the shop while I'm gone, and I'll order some lunch for us when I get back. Unfortunately, my car is acting up," she lied. "I need to take the bus, but I'll bring Bella with me. She'll enjoy the ride." Vivian quickly grabbed her things, called Bella, and they left the shop.

Instead of heading straight down Third Street to the bus stop, Vivian and Bella walked behind the shop to the next road over and waited for the bus on Beverly Boulevard. Vivian couldn't remember the last time she rode the bus, but she felt safer taking a different form of transportation today. Between the man hanging around the post office a few nights and the police car parked across the street for a while last night, she hoped leaving her Renault in the alley would deter anyone from following her and finding out where she was going.

The bus finally arrived. Vivian carried Bella up the steps and sat in one of the front seats with Bella in her lap. After transferring to a connecting line, they got off at Pearl Street and walked down the quiet residential road.

They were several houses away when Bella started running down the narrow sidewalk and disappeared up the stone path leading to the small brick home. As Vivian walked up the sidewalk, Bella was on the front steps, scratching at the door and wagging her tail.

The door opened, and Bella raced inside.

Arthur stood in the doorway dressed in a lime-green sweater and tan slacks with his pure white hair neatly combed back. "Good morning, Vivian. This is a surprise."

"I'm sorry for showing up unannounced. Do you have time to talk?"

"Of course, I do. Come inside." After he closed the door behind her, he bent down to pet Bella, who was excitedly running circles around his feet. "Did you want a cup of coffee? I just made a fresh pot."

"Yes. I can help myself."

"Nonsense. Have a seat. No cream or sugar, right?"

Vivian nodded and sat on the couch. Bella pranced right along behind Arthur into the kitchen and came back with a dog biscuit sticking out of her mouth.

"Here we go," Arthur said. He handed Vivian the coffee mug and sat in one of the armchairs. "So, what's on your mind?"

She took a deep breath. "It probably won't surprise you that I didn't heed the advice you gave me the last time I visited."

"That was four months ago, Vivian, and any advice I give you is merely a suggestion. You're old enough to make your own decisions. Tell me what happened."

"You're not going to like it. I contacted Joey Carnival in New York. I knew he had some connections in Los Angeles, and he gave me the name of a man who helped me track down Elliott Kimball."

Arthur took a sip of his coffee. "You know better than anyone how dangerous it is to ask a favor from Joey, but I read in the paper that the police killed Kimball in a shootout, and they closed George's case. Let me guess. You were at Bunker Hill Saturday night, weren't you?"

"Elliott Kimball didn't kill George, but I think I know who did, and Joey is the least of my problems right now..." Briefly, she told him about going to the hotel, running into Preston, and finding Tilly Trimble dead along with the photograph of her and George on the coffee table. She explained about the mayor's affair with Tilly, going to the courthouse to watch Captain Kynette's trial, and driving to the docks at Marina del Rey. "Captain Kynette killed George. I'm sure of it, but I think I opened up Pandora's box."

She waited for Arthur to say something, anything, but he just sat there for a few minutes, taking his sweet time to respond while she was crawling out of her skin since she had so much more to tell him.

"If you're stepping on the mayor's toes, Vivian, then you're right. That's more dangerous than owing Joey a favor, especially now. I just heard on the radio that a few charges against Captain Kynette were dropped, and he's probably feeling pretty confident that the mayor will make sure he goes free. Therefore, retaliation is the only thing on his mind. Has anyone threatened you?"

"Yes, but in such a ludicrous way, I can't believe the mayor is behind it." Vivian opened her carry bag and pulled out her sketches. "I received a ticket to a movie premiere the other day. I thought one of my new clients sent it as a gift. When I got to the Liberty Theatre yesterday afternoon, Preston Stone was the only person in the audience. The movie was just a short, seven-minute clip, but it had a very threatening message, although, for the life of me, I can't figure out what that message is outside of the fact that someone plans on killing me and possibly Preston. I've sketched a couple of scenes. Here, take a look at these."

Arthur set his coffee mug down and took the sketches from her. "You haven't lost your touch. These are extremely detailed sketches. Tell me about the content of the movie."

As she gave him a recap, she pointed to the sketch of the woman wearing a blazer exactly like hers, which was missing from her boutique, and the man's scarf with Preston Stone's initials. "The last few sketches were the most significant. The coins were the focal point of the entire movie, but I don't know anything about any coins."

"Preston Stone...isn't he the rich fella your sister was seeing just before she moved back to New York?"

"Yes, and I know what you're going to ask next. I have no idea why Preston arrived at the hotel room when I did, either. I thought he might have killed Tilly Trimble, but I'm convinced the mayor had one of his men kill her, just like he had Captain Kynette kill George out of jealousy."

Arthur studied the drawings. "This movie doesn't sound like the mayor's handiwork. Are you sure Preston Stone wasn't behind it?"

"As much as I dislike him, I can't believe he's that good of an actor. He seemed genuinely surprised to see me at the theater when I walked in and shocked at the contents of the movie. Besides, he was depicted as a victim, too. Since his family is extremely wealthy, I considered the possibility that the coins symbolized a large amount of money and extortion was behind it. But if that were the case, why involve me at all? In the movie, the coins were in my possession, and Preston was searching for them."

"Perhaps the coins represent something else, Vivian. If the entire purpose of the movie was to force you to hand over these valuable coins to them, how would you do that? They didn't give you any sort of instructions, timeframe, or drop-off point. I would've expected that to be included. It sounds to me like the movie was more of a warning than a threat."

Vivian stood up and walked across the room. "Maybe you're right. Carole and I went to Perino's Restaurant last night. Joe Shaw cornered me in the hallway and tried to intimidate me. There was definitely a hidden message behind his words and demeanor."

"The Shaw brothers might know this Trimble woman had called you shortly before her death, and they're worried she told you something that could damage them."

"Like the fact that the mayor arranged George's death," Vivian stated. "I wondered if that was the reason Tilly wanted to meet with me. Maybe the mayor thinks she told Preston the same thing. That would explain why they're targeting both of us. It also proves the mayor's guilt."

"Do you still have your Beretta pistol?"

"I packed it away somewhere when I moved here."

"Carry it in your purse for a while, just to be safe. I'm also going to call a friend of mine. I'm sure he'd be willing to watch over you until this blows over."

When Vivian turned around to look at him, a small picture hanging on the kitchen wall caught her eye. "No, don't trouble him. I don't want anyone following me around." She wandered into the kitchen as she spoke, then stood there gazing at the framed charcoal portrait of her mother. "Where did you get this picture, Arthur? I've never seen it here before."

"I always put it away when you stopped by," he told her. "I didn't want to upset you, but you caught me off guard today."

"Did Uncle Reggie give it to you?"

"Yes...after the funeral. The three of us were inseparable as kids." Arthur set the sketches down and went into the kitchen to stand behind her. "As I said, your artistic ability is exceptional. You were only sixteen years old when you sketched that picture."

She reached up to touch the portrait. "My mother was very pretty, wasn't she?"

"Ellie was a beautiful woman. You're the spitting image of her, you know." He placed his hand on her shoulder. "Vivian, I'm sorry about what George did to you. I didn't know him, but from what you told me, I didn't see this coming. Why don't you and Bella stay with me for a few days? You'll be safe, and I won't have to worry about you."

She shook her head while gazing at the portrait.

He grumbled under his breath. "I'm not sure why you came here to tell me all this if you won't let me help you."

Vivian turned to him. "I'm not going to run away and hide again."

"You haven't been in hiding," Arthur sighed. "You simply closed the door to your past and came here to start a new life. There's a difference."

"Is there, Arthur? Why do I feel like the past is just repeating itself?"

"Because George turned out to be a damn louse! He's the reason you're involved in this. You could dig deeper into what attracted you to George, and why you didn't see who he really was underneath. You could spin your wheels for years trying to figure that out, but you know better than anyone that some people are just that good at concealing their true selves. And then there are times when we don't want to see the truth, even when it's staring us in the face. If you're hiding from anyone, Vivian, maybe it's yourself. You may not want my advice or heed it, but here it is anyway. Take charge of your life again, keep that pistol within reach, and don't let anyone else make you feel like a victim."

As she absorbed his words, her expression eased. "Thank you, Arthur, and not only for the advice but for being honest with me. You're one of the few people I trust. That's why I came here, and what I love most about you." She leaned over and kissed his cheek. "Do you have a telephone book?"

"It's on the kitchen counter. Why?"

"I'm going to find out who had access to the Liberty Theatre yesterday afternoon." She went over and flipped through the pages. Then she went into the living room to gather her things. "I'll call you later."

"Watch your back, Vivian."

She nodded and left with Bella to catch the bus heading for Sunset Boulevard. The main office for the Liberty Theatre was located on Sierra Drive, right around the corner from the theater. Within twenty-five minutes, she and Bella walked into the office building and spoke to the front receptionist, who directed her to the manager's office down the hall.

Vivian decided to carry Bella to keep her quiet. She noted the man's name on the door, entered the office, and approached his secretary. "Good morning. My name is...Missus Ramsey. I wondered if I could speak with Mister Callahan for a moment?"

"Do you have an appointment?" she asked.

"No, but it should only take a moment."

The young woman picked up the phone and spoke to the manager. "You may go right in, Missus Ramsey."

Vivian thanked her and entered the office. The gentleman sitting behind the desk was an older man. "Good morning, Mister Callahan. Thank you for seeing me on such short notice."

"Certainly. How can I help you?"

"A friend of mine attended a short film at the Liberty Theatre yesterday afternoon. I wondered if you could tell me who was in charge of the production."

He started laughing. "It must have been one hell of a movie. Excuse my language, but you're the second person to ask about it. I have no idea who produced it, but Mister Preston Stone rented the theater for the afternoon. He could answer your questions better than I can."

14

New Beginning

Vivian headed straight home and got off the bus on Third Street, one block away from the boutique. She was in disbelief and furious as hell. As much as she despised Preston and the type of man he represented, she had thought he was completely innocent in both Tilly's murder and at the movie theater. She even defended him to Arthur, like an idiot, but he'd tricked her, too.

She was convinced now that Preston was guilty as sin. Whether he was good buddies with the mayor or not, he either killed Tilly Trimble himself, or he was with the person who did. That's why he was at the hotel and followed her up to Tilly's room, and why he sent her on her way so quickly. And that demented movie was exactly what she and Arthur had determined...a warning for her to stay out of it.

As soon as she reached the front door of the boutique, she caught a strong whiff of pastrami in the air. It was going on eleven-thirty, and she'd promised Nora that they would have lunch together. She and Bella walked across the alley to Martino's. Vivian had the garden party in a few hours, and she didn't want to eat a big lunch. So, she ordered a pastrami sandwich with Swiss on rye for Nora and a cup of minestrone for herself.

While she waited for the order, she wandered over to the front window and stood there angry with herself, Preston, George, the mayor's brother, and everyone else involved in this. That's when she noticed a patrol car slowly pulling up the side street next to the post office. It turned at the corner and parked directly across the street.

Vivian moved closer to the glass and caught a sly grin. The passenger window was rolled down, and she recognized the police officer sitting there. "Tony, I'll be right back!" she called out. "Stay here, Bella." Boldly, she walked outside, marched across the street, and approached the patrol car. "Hello, Officer Smythe."

He sat upright in his seat and straightened his cap.

She held a sweet smile on him. "You probably don't remember me, but I hoped to run into you one day. I wanted to thank you. I'm Vivian Steele. You helped me the night my husband was killed during a robbery on Hollywood Boulevard about six months ago. I was beside myself that night, and I'll never forget your kindness."

"Yes, ma'am, I remember. How...how are you doing?"

"It hasn't been easy, but life goes on, doesn't it?" She leaned down and peered at the officer in the driver's seat. "Good afternoon, Officer..."

"Peterson, ma'am."

"Why don't I buy lunch for both of you at Martino's Delicatessen across the street to show my gratitude? I just placed my order. They make the best pastrami sandwiches in the city."

"Uh...no, we're fine. Thanks," Officer Peterson said.

"It's unusual to see a patrol car in this neighborhood," she went on innocently. "Has there been trouble in the area?" She stared at both of them, waiting for an answer.

"Not at all. We were just passing through," Officer Smythe told her.

"Well, that's a relief. I'll let you get back to work. Have a wonderful day, officers." Vivian walked away, knowing she had made them very uncomfortable. They were whispering to each other right now and before she even reached the curb, the patrol car pulled away.

After she picked up her order at Martino's, she and Bella returned to the boutique through the alley. But Vivian opened the side door, and Bella started growling. Henry from the shoe store across the street was wandering around in the back room.

She stepped inside, and Nora was nowhere in sight. "Henry, can I help you?"

He turned around and his cheeks flushed. "Oh, Miss Steele, I...I'm waiting to talk to Nora. She told me to always use the side door instead of coming through the front, so I don't bother the customers."

Vivian went over and peeked into the display room. Nora was standing at the cash register, ringing up a customer sale. She waved to Nora to let her know she had returned. Then she tossed her purse and carry bag on the small counter next to the sink and set their lunch on the table next to a shoebox. "What's this?"

"It's a pair of single-strapped Mary Jane shoes," Henry told her. "A salesman came by the store to sell us a few new styles. I was hoping Nora would try these on and let me know what she thought. The manufacturer added extra padding in the soles for more comfort and longer wear. They're more expensive than the shoes we've been carrying, and we didn't want to make a hasty decision."

Vivian noticed Henry's shoes. "I've never seen you wear two-toned shoes before."

He looked down at his feet and chuckled. "Yeah, my shoes are usually more formal while working. The salesman wanted me to try these out. They're made by the Cobbs & Howe Company. You can tell by their signature broguing, which are the perforations around the top of the shoe that look like the wings of a bird. That's how they got the name *wingtip*s."

He'd piqued her interest. "Henry, would you mind taking a look at this?" She went over and pulled out her sketch of the man in the movie wearing the two-toned shoes out of her bag. "Is there anything you can tell me about those shoes?"

Henry took the sketch from her and studied it. "This is a great drawing. First, there are quarter brogues, full brogues like the ones I'm wearing, and longwing brogues where the broguing goes all the way around the shoe."

"I see." Vivian was beginning to understand why Nora didn't seem interested in dating Henry. He was a sweet young man, but much too focused on his work.

"These are two-toned longwing brogues, but do you see the four single perforations in the center above the wings? There's no doubt about it. These were custom-made at Robertson's over in Malibu. That's their signature design and the only place that sells them."

"Really. That's very helpful. Thank you, Henry."

Nora rushed into the back room excitedly. "Did you buy pastrami sandwiches, Vivian? That's all I could smell when I was taking care of Missus Wagner. What are you doing here, Henry?"

While he explained about the salesman and asked Nora to try on the shoes, Vivian put her sketch back into her bag and sat down. She glanced over at the garment rack.

Someone had waltzed in here and taken her red blazer right off the rack either during working hours or when the shop was closed. There wasn't any sign of forced entry, but the locks on the front and side doors were an older design. When they finished lunch, she was going to call the locksmith and have him install a more secure system that included a deadbolt for both the front and back doors, along with the door to her apartment.

"These shoes are comfortable and pretty, too," Nora said, sticking them back into the shoebox. "If they weren't too expensive, I'd buy them. Now skedaddle, Henry, so we can eat our lunch." She joined Vivian at the table and waited for Henry to leave. "Did everything go well this morning?"

Vivian handed her the sandwich. "Yes, it did."

"I'm glad. Missus Wagner wanted to know when we were going to carry men's clothing. She said there isn't a good men's shop in Beverly Hills."

Vivian smiled. "We have enough to keep us busy, which is why I've decided to hire a salesclerk whether I end up with a department store contract or not. This week has been crazy, and I've felt terrible leaving you here and at the market by yourself for so many hours. If your roommate is interested, have her stop by."

"I know you've had a lot going on, and I haven't minded working alone, but I've been hoping to spend more time helping you instead of just waiting on the customers. You have the charity event later today, so I'll tell Nancy to come by tomorrow. She'll be so excited."

"Speaking of the charity event, I also decided to close the boutique at three o'clock today. I'll pay you for your regular hours. It's the least I can do to thank you for all your help. We both could use a break. We might lose some sales, but we're backed up with orders as it is, and I plan on working all weekend to make up for it. I'd love for you to come with me to the garden party if you don't have anything else to do."

"Thank you for the offer, but I was going to ask you if I could leave a little early today," Nora said. "If you're sure about closing the shop, that will work out great. I met someone while I was waiting at the bus stop this morning. We started talking and laughing and before I knew it, I missed the bus, so he gave me a ride to work. He also asked me if I wanted to see Kenny Baker sing at Ocean Park Beach later this afternoon. Can you believe it? You know how much I adore him."

"That's wonderful, Nora. I'm happy for you."

The two of them finished their lunch and worked until three o'clock. As soon as Nora left, Vivian closed the boutique and headed into the storage room before going upstairs. She dug around in the boxes, found her Beretta handgun, and tucked it into her purse.

Upstairs, Vivian took a leisure bath and thought about her conversation with Arthur. He was right about taking charge of her life, which she realized she'd lost when she moved here. Perhaps even deliberately in her desperate quest to lead a normal life. That would explain so much, like why she blindly jumped at the chance to marry George and turned the other cheek with his frequent nights out and weekends away. And since his death, she'd spent an obsessive amount of time focused on tracking his killer.

She needed to find a better balance between who she was, what she wanted, and what she needed. But all of that and whatever she decided to do next about the events going on around her was going to wait until tomorrow. Today, she intended to relax, forget about the rest, and have a good time, for once.

Vivian put on her makeup and wore a sleeveless, slightly low-cut summer dress that she'd made from a shimmery silk material in multiple pastel colors. She always dressed more conservatively, but she was feeling a little risqué this afternoon.

When she was finished, she lifted her hand and stared at the diamond ring and gold wedding band on her finger. George didn't deserve to die, but Arthur was right. George was a louse, and she was glad she found out what kind of man he was rather than spend the rest of her life grieving for him.

With that, she pulled the rings off her finger and stuck them into her jewelry box. Then she marched into the living room, snatched her wedding picture on the end table, and shoved it into the top drawer.

15

Garden Party

A line of cars waited to use the valet service in the circular driveway in front of Carole's home. Vivian drove a little further and pulled into the grassy lot that was designated for parking. Before she got out of the car, she took the handgun out of her purse and stuck it underneath the front seat for safekeeping.

Then she and Bella headed for the side door of the house. Suzanne greeted them, and Vivian spoke with her for a few minutes. She thanked her for watching the pups and walked along the slate path to the yard behind the home. Along the way, Vivian could hear soft background music playing and the low roar of people talking and laughing.

She smiled when she saw the meticulously tended yard and beautiful gardens. In true Carole fashion, everything looked breathtaking, the tasteful decorations, lovely floral arrangements, and the elegantly dressed staff she'd hired to pass around food and drink. The four-piece band was set up on the patio. Long tables covered with white tablecloths lined the lattice fence edging a portion of the yard. Two were for the appetizers and canapés, another served as a makeshift bar, and a smaller table at the end held a decorative box for donations.

As Vivian expected, she knew quite a few of the guests in attendance, including current customers of hers and those in the acting business who were either customers or acquaintances she'd met through Carole. So, she spent a good amount of time chatting with several people as she slowly made her way through the crowd. She even ran into Wanda Schwinn, a very sweet woman who had worked with George at the bank, and they talked for quite a while.

Vivian finally spotted Carole standing by one of the buffet tables, talking with Myrna Loy. She didn't want to interrupt them, but as soon as Carole saw her, she excused herself and hurried over. "What took you so long?"

"You've outdone yourself, Carole," Vivian said. "Everything looks beautiful, and what a wonderful turnout."

Carole clutched her arm. "Yes, it's lovely, but listen to me. You'll never guess who's here."

Clark suddenly walked over to them, wrapped his arm around Carole, and flashed Vivian a dashing grin. "Hello, Vivian, don't you look pretty as a peach today?"

"Thank you, Clark."

Carole glanced up at him. "Did you mend fences with Spencer? Myrna said the two of you haven't spoken since you finished filming *Test Pilots* with her back in March."

"Naw, he's still sore at me. I tried to smooth things over with him, but he's stubborn as a mule. He'll get over it. I ran into Selznick and his wife. He's trying to twist my arm about accepting the role in that Civil War film, the part that Gary Cooper turned down. I guess they have fourteen hundred women auditioning for the female lead."

"I told you that you should take the part," Carole said. "I even bought the book for you, but you didn't even look at it." She turned to Vivian. "They're making a movie based on Margaret Mitchell's novel, *Gone With the Wind*, and they want Clark to play Rhett Butler. You read the book, didn't you? I thought it was fantastic."

"It's one of my favorites," Vivian agreed.

Clark laughed. "Yeah, well, Coop swears it's going to bomb at the box office, but I'll think about it."

"Clark, would you mind getting us both a glass of champagne?" Carole asked.

He looked at the two of them and lifted a brow. "I can take a hint, ladies. You're trying to get rid of me, aren't you?"

"Just for a few minutes."

He laughed. "Okay, honey, I'll take my time."

Carole waited until he was out of earshot. "Vivian, that no good David is here. Can you believe it?"

"George's friend? Why would he be invited to this?"

"I wondered about that, too, and found out he came with his boss who owns the real estate company. He's standing right over there at the first buffet table."

"Is Preston here?" Vivian asked as he was the one person she wanted to avoid at all costs.

"I saw him earlier, but we didn't have a chance to talk. I've been keeping a lookout for Gary Rutherford, but no sign of him."

"Did I hear someone mention my name?" Gary asked as he joined them. "Good afternoon, ladies. This is quite an elaborate event. Thank you for inviting me, Carole. It's good to see you, Vivian. You look lovely this afternoon."

Clark returned with their drinks, and Carole introduced him to Gary. The four of them talked for a while, but soon, the director of the children's charity stood on the patio. She asked the band to stop playing and quieted everyone down so she could say a few words. Her speech included a brief description of their organization, and she explained how the donations would be distributed. She finished by thanking all the guests for coming, and she asked for a round of applause for Carole for her generosity in hosting the event.

As soon as the band resumed playing and guests went back to socializing, Vivian noticed Preston heading their way. Carole noticed him, too, and nudged her. "Viv, why don't you take Gary over to the buffet table for something to eat?"

Gladly, Vivian left with Gary and, for the next hour, the two of them had quite an enjoyable time together. They sampled a few of the delicious appetizers, including pineapple-ginger shrimp cocktail, oysters on the half shell, crab salad, and strawberry tortes. Afterward, they took their drinks and slowly strolled along the stone pathway through the gardens.

On their way back, they stopped at the edge of the path before joining the others. "So, tell me, Gary, how did you become a wholesale buyer?" Vivian asked.

He chuckled. "It's a pretty humorous story since I never had any interest in fashion in my younger years. My heart was set on following in my father's footsteps by becoming a lawyer. As soon as I graduated high school, I applied to the University at Berkeley and..."

Vivian listened intently to Gary at first, but she became distracted by one of the waiters who was walking around the side of the house to the backyard. The young man was buttoning his white shirt and tying a black apron around his waist as though he'd just arrived. He went over to the bar and grabbed one of the serving trays. Then he set a single glass of champagne on it. All the while, he was acting strangely and frequently glanced around.

"I couldn't refuse the owner's offer," Gary went on. "So, I quit college and started working as a salesman in his store. Within months, he opened another shop in the city and promoted me to manager. It just kept escalating from there."

"Buchmann's is a very elite men's shop," Vivian muttered.

As Gary finished the rest of his story, Vivian continued watching the waiter and couldn't believe her eyes. The young man pulled something out of his pants pocket. After taking another look around, he poured the contents of it into the champagne glass and carried the single glass on the tray through the crowd.

"When did you get into fashion design?" Gary asked.

"What? Oh, I'm sorry, Gary. I...I think Carole needs my help with something. I'll be right back."

She left his side and walked over to find the waiter. She caught sight of him making his way through the crowd. He headed toward Preston, who was talking with a few other guests, but instead of passing by him, the young man deliberately poked his elbow out and knocked Preston's arm hard enough to send his drink flying into the air and landing on the ground.

Vivian couldn't hear what the waiter said to Preston, but he was obviously apologizing profusely while Preston laughed it off and assured him that he was fine. Then the waiter handed Preston the glass of champagne from his tray. He apologized again and disappeared into the crowd.

Vivian stood there another moment in disbelief, then she hurried over to Preston and roped her arm through his, surprising the daylights out of him. She smiled at the other guests. "Excuse us. I'm going to steal Preston away for just a minute." She yanked on his arm and dragged him with her. As they went, she snatched the glass out of his hand.

"What's going on, Vivian?"

She set the glass on the bar and led him a couple of feet away. "Your champagne is spiked with something."

He scowled at her. "What are you talking about?"

"That waiter poured some sort of liquid or powder into it, and he purposely bumped into you, so you'd drop your glass."

It took Preston a moment to comprehend what she'd said. "Where did he go?"

"He's long gone by now. Don't ask me why, but I was more concerned with stopping you from drinking the champagne than trying to stop him from leaving."

"What did he look like?" Preston asked, glancing around.

"Early twenties, sandy blonde hair, five foot ten, maybe, and skinny as a rail. I'll let you deal with it. I've got to get back to the other guests."

"Hold on, Vivian. We need to talk."

She glared at him. "About what?"

"I know what you're thinking, but I didn't have anything to do with that movie."

"That's not what I heard," she said, straightening her back. "I talked to the manager, and he said you rented the theater for the afternoon. I don't know what the blazes you're up to, Preston, or who you're working for, but I don't want any part of it. Just leave me alone." Vivian turned around to leave, but an older man was standing behind her at the bar now, and he picked up the glass of champagne to drink it. She panicked, dove forward, and snatched it out of his hand. "Excuse me, sir! This is *my* drink."

"Geez, pardon me, lady." The man grumbled something and left.

"I'll take the glass," Preston told her. "I want to find out what the waiter put in it."

Vivian handed it to him. "How are you going to do that?"

He leaned over the bar, poured the champagne into one of the sterling silver cocktail shakers, and put the top on. "Thanks for your help."

She watched him for another moment then walked away.

"Vivian!" Preston called out. He waited for her to turn around. "Where are the coins?"

She stood there, staring at him.

"You don't know anything about them, do you?" he asked as he approached her. "That's what I thought. Okay, now I'm going to insist that we go someplace private to talk. Did you tell Carole about the movie?"

Vivian shook her head.

"Good. Why don't we wrap things up here, make our excuses, and you can follow me back to my parents' estate? Or better yet, leave your car here and ride with me."

"I'm not going anywhere with you."

"Oh, give it a rest, Vivian." He held up the cocktail shaker. "You might be next. We're both in danger. Do you want to know why?"

16

Bella & Boris

Vivian walked through the crowd at a turtle's pace, thinking about what had just transpired. She didn't trust Preston one darn bit, but he'd succeeded in convincing her to drive to Santa Monica to listen to what he had to say. She just hoped she wasn't making a big mistake.

By the time she spotted Gary, he was standing at the buffet table, talking with another guest. She had truly enjoyed his company and didn't want to just disappear into thin air without a word to him. But she also didn't want to fumble around like an idiot, giving him some lame excuse as to why she was leaving so early. Lying to Carole would be tough enough since her best friend could see right through her.

Still, he deserved some sort of explanation, especially since he was instrumental in her getting the Bullock's contract. Vivian made her way over to him and waited until he finished his conversation. Then, she used work as an excuse and explained that she needed to finish an important client's order and deliver it first thing in the morning. Thankfully, he understood and said he was going to leave soon as well.

"Why don't we meet for drinks at Cole's after work tomorrow?" he asked. "I'm meeting the executives in the morning, so I might have some good news for you."

"That sounds lovely," she replied almost mindlessly. "I'll meet you there at five o'clock."

"I look forward to it."

She wished him a good evening and went in search of Carole next. She found her near the patio amid what seemed to be a deep conversation with Spencer Tracy, and Clark was making his way over to them. With a twinge of guilt, she decided she'd rather apologize to Carole tomorrow rather than wait to talk with her now.

She made her way over to Preston, waltzed by him, and whispered, "I'm ready to go." She continued around to the side door and after she thanked Suzanne again, she gathered Bella.

As they walked to her car, Vivian noticed Preston heading for his sporty red Jaguar not far away. Without acknowledging him, she and Bella got into her car. Vivian put her gun back into her purse and waited for Preston to leave first. Then she slowly pulled out onto the road to follow behind him.

That's when she heard Carole calling to her. Vivian glanced over and saw Carole standing in the grass on the side of the house with her hands on her hips, watching her drive away. Vivian stepped on the gas and sped down the road.

She followed Preston down Santa Monica Boulevard the entire way, and within twenty minutes, they arrived at the massive estate on the beach. Vivian slowly passed by it and despite everything she'd heard about the Stone Estate, she couldn't get over the enormity of the mansion.

Preston pulled into the open concrete carport on the south side of the home and motioned for her to park next to him. As soon as Vivian opened the car door, Bella jumped down and raced over to Preston excitedly, as though she knew him well.

"Who's your companion?" he asked as he bent down to pet her.

Vivian scowled. "Bella usually doesn't like strangers."

"She's smart. She knows I carry a few treats in my pocket." Preston gave one to her. "We'll go outside to the back patio. There's someone here who's sure to keep Bella entertained." He grabbed the cocktail shaker from his car and led the way to the front door and into the foyer.

They walked through the sitting room and dining room before they reached a short hallway. Vivian looked around in awe, admiring the beautiful Victorian furniture and gorgeous oil paintings decorating the walls. Finally, they entered a large living area, and a distinguished older gentleman, formally dressed in a black suit and bowtie, was standing by the closed double glass doors, staring outside.

"I'll take it from here, Gunther," Preston told him. "Was he any trouble?"

"Not really, sir. I tried to feed him, but he refused to get out of the water." Gunther turned around and saw Vivian. "Good evening, Miss."

"This is Vivian Steele," Preston introduced. "Vivian, I'd like you to meet Gunther. If it weren't for him, this entire estate would come crashing down around us."

"Nice to meet you," she said.

"If there's nothing else, sir, I'll get back to my regular duties."

"One more thing, Gunther." Preston handed him the cocktail shaker. "I need you to..."

"Take it to your study? Of course, sir."

Gunther headed for the hallway, but before he left the room, he glanced back at Vivian again. She watched him and wondered about it. There was something in the older man's expression when he saw her there. His light eyes widened for a second as though he recognized her, or she spurred some sort of memory.

Preston opened the glass doors. "I'll meet you on the patio, Vivian. I'm going to make us both a drink and don't be alarmed when you see Boris lounging in the pool. He's perfectly harmless."

Not knowing what to expect, she picked Bella up and slowly walked out to the patio. Immediately, she spotted Boris lying in the water on the top step of the pool. "Oh, my..."

Bella saw him, too, and started squirming in Vivian's arms, wanting to get down.

"Are you sure he's harmless?" Vivian called out.

Before Preston could answer her, Bella wiggled around so much that Vivian was afraid she'd drop her. She set her on the ground, and Bella raced over to the edge of the pool, wagging her tail and softly yipping at Boris. Vivian followed behind her to make sure Bella was safe.

Leisurely, Boris got out of the pool and shook himself off, then he and Bella started sniffing each other. Vivian watched them closely, and she began petting Boris. "He's very sweet, isn't he?"

Preston handed her a scotch on the rocks. "Boris is big, but he's gentle as a lamb. While the two of them get to know each other, let's have a seat."

Vivian kept an eye on Bella and sat at the nearby table. "I don't plan on staying long. I want to know about the coins."

Preston leaned back in his chair. "First, why don't you tell me why you're under police surveillance?"

She glared at him. "Really, Preston? You brought me all the way over here just to play games? What makes you think I'm under surveillance?"

"After you refused to answer my phone calls last evening, I drove by your building and saw a patrol car parked across the street."

She took a sip of her drink. "All right. I think the mayor is worried Tilly Trimble told me something damaging about him before I went to the hotel, and the police are watching me."

"Did she?"

"No, but after I saw the photograph of her and my husband in her hotel room, I found out the mayor was having an affair with her, too. I'm convinced the mayor arranged George's death out of jealousy last fall, and Tilly was going to inform me about it. That's why he hired either you or someone else to kill her. There, all my cards are on the table, Preston."

"Not all of them. I thought Elliott Kimball shot your husband. He's not affiliated with the mayor."

"Kimball was right-handed. The gunman was left-handed like Captain Kynette, who is strongly linked to the mayor."

"Ah, that explains why you were at Kynette's trial."

She bolted to her feet. "So, you've been following me, too. I recognize Boris now. He was with the man standing in front of the post office a few nights the past week. This is a waste of time. I'm leaving."

"Sit down, Vivian. I had Freddie follow you, but not for the reasons you think. And I didn't kill Tilly Trimble. I also didn't have a dinner date with her that night, but let's save that for later and talk about the coins. Chester Willoughby was a good friend of my father's. He passed away last week, and when his attorney, who is also the executor of his estate, opened up Chester's safe deposit box at Bank of America, his rare collection of coins was missing. A very valuable collection, I might add. It's worth at least two million dollars."

Vivian sat down, listening intently. "Go on."

"The attorney is hoping to recoup the coins before reporting it to the police, and I agreed to help him. Six people had access to the safe deposit box, three employees at the bank and Chester's three children."

"George..." she muttered.

Preston nodded. "He wasn't at the top of my list of suspects until yesterday after watching the movie. Someone else discovered the coins were missing, and he's convinced George took them. That was the whole concept of the film. He thinks you have the coins now, and he knows I'm looking for them."

"George died six months ago. Why would he think George stole them?"

"We don't know if the coins were taken recently or a year ago. This guy might have done his own research and narrowed it down to George. Maybe he's trying to take my focus off the real thief, or perhaps, and this would be my guess, George stole the coins and confided in someone about his theft before he died. Someone he was close to, like Tilly Trimble, and recently, she shared that information with our film producer before he killed her."

Vivian stood up again, but this time she wandered over to Bella and Boris, who were contentedly lying side-by-side on the patio not far from the pool. A week ago, she would have argued tooth and nail against anyone who accused George of a crime, but everything was different now. "If George stole them, I can't imagine where they would be. After he died, I packed all of our things and moved into the apartment above my boutique. There weren't any coins."

"Do you own a thirty-two caliber Beretta pistol?" Preston asked.

She glanced over at her purse on the chair.

"I thought so," Preston said. "That's the type of gun that was used to kill Tilly."

"What are you saying?"

"After you left the hotel, I found several items sprinkled around that would have easily framed you for her murder had the police arrived first. If they found that gun in your possession, it would have sealed your conviction."

"What items?"

He hesitated. "Similar to the photograph you found."

Vivian thought about it. "You realize that everything you've told me points to the mayor, between his relationship with Tilly, his jealousy over George, and planting evidence against me. Why would Tilly wait six months to tell him about the coin collection, though?" Vivian wandered back to the table. "Unless she wasn't sure George took the coins until she found out they were missing."

"That brings us back around to who leaked the information. Only a handful of us knew the coins were stolen."

"A handful of who?" Vivian asked.

Preston grinned at her. "Getting back to the mayor, he's guilty of a lot of different crimes, and he might have arranged Tilly Trimble's death, but patience and subtlety aren't his strong suits. He usually takes what he wants without caring about the consequences and wouldn't bother to make a movie to get his point across. You're probably right that he instructed Captain Kynette to kill your husband. That's more his style. It was your visit to the courthouse that alerted him that you suspect what really happened."

Vivian sat down and took another sip of her drink. "Preston, if this mystery man, whoever he is, wants the coins and thinks I have them, why hasn't he given me any instructions on how to give them to him? He went to all the trouble of making that violent seven-minute film, and the only message was that he's willing to kill us for the coins."

"I don't know, but right now, my top priority is finding the person who stole the coins in the first place and retrieving them. That would put an end to all of this. If it's any comfort, we both may be targets, but I'm in more danger than you are since I'm just in the way. As long as he thinks you have the coins, you're fairly safe."

"Now that you brought that up, I'm curious about the glass of champagne. How are you going to find out what the waiter put in it?"

"I have some equipment upstairs in my study to test for different substances."

"Then I suggest you either test the champagne soon or transfer it to a glass container. Depending upon the type of substance the waiter put into it, the amount of silver in the cocktail shaker could react with it, altering the properties and possibly turning it into a deadly inhalant."

Preston fell silent for a moment as he gazed at her. "You obviously have experience in more than just fashion design. Where did you live before you came to Los Angeles?"

She smiled at him. "Let's save that for later when you tell me the *real* reason you went to Tilly Trimble's hotel room."

Preston laughed. "Fair enough. Come on, why don't we go upstairs and find out how long it would have taken that champagne to kill me?"

17

Mind Games

Bella and Boris followed the two of them up the wide split marble staircase that continued higher for several open levels. "I sketched a few of the scenes from the movie," Vivian said, but she stopped for a second when she noticed the magnificent crystal chandelier hanging from the ceiling far above their heads. "I don't believe the size of this place. How many floors are there, four or five?"

"Six," Preston told her. "What about your sketches?"

"I drew a picture of our mystery man's wing-tip shoes at the end of the movie where he's picking up the coins off the floor. Henry works at his father's shoe store across the street, and I showed the drawing to him. He said the shoes were custom made at Robertson's shoe store in Malibu."

"I'll give them a call tomorrow. What else did you sketch?"

"The woman wearing the blazer with my business logo on the pocket, which was taken right off the rack in the back room of my shop. I gather the neck scarf with your initials also disappeared?"

"That was his way of letting us know he's in control, and we're not even safe in our own homes."

"Well, that's not comforting at all."

Preston opened the door to his study on the second floor. "Did you have your locks changed?"

"The locksmith is coming tomorrow at ten o'clock." As she entered the room, Boris brushed by her and headed for the balcony with Bella hot on his heels. Vivian smiled and went with them. The two of them lay down close to one another while she leaned over the railing and gazed at the breathtaking view of the sun setting over the ocean. "Let me guess. You're an only child, aren't you, Preston?"

He opened the oak hutch and set up his chemistry apparatus. "What difference does it make?"

"None, I suppose, except that explains..." Vivian cut her own words off, realizing how insulting it would sound. She wandered back inside and noticed the small stack of folders on his desk with George's name written on the first tab. "You've certainly done your research. How did you come upon these files?"

"Chester's attorney gathered them for me."

She eyed Preston. "Tell me again why you're involved in this?"

"I'm doing it as a favor to my father."

Vivian knew he was lying, or at the very least, not telling her everything. "I suppose you have a separate folder on me?"

"As I said, your husband wasn't a main suspect until yesterday."

"Then why were you having someone follow me?"

"We're back to that again?" Preston chuckled. "Last Friday, I was driving through the city and spotted you on the corner of Alameda and First Street talking with...well, let's just say, someone I wouldn't expect you to know. I wondered what you were up to."

She knew he was referring to one of her meetings with Lucky and wondered, herself, what Preston was doing in that part of the city. "That sounds pretty flimsy."

"It seemed out of character for you until I found out that you were at Bunker Hill on Saturday night. I realized you were looking for your husband's killer."

She shrugged her shoulders and flipped through the other folders. "I assume Chester Willoughby, Jr. and John Willoughby are the man's sons."

"Both of them have been working at their father's investment firm for several years and will inherit the ownership of the company now, along with their share of Chester's wealth, which is significant all on its own. I've done thorough background checks on all three siblings and their spouses, and as far as I can tell, they're a very loyal family."

"So, they're unlikely suspects, although not out of the question if one of them got greedy. Who is Carol McCarthy?"

"Chester Willoughby's married daughter. Her husband works at the firm, too."

"Here's Wanda Schwinn's file, the bank teller. She's a very sweet woman and wouldn't have anything to do with this. I'm sure of it." Vivian picked up the next file. "I can't say the same thing for Thomas Goldman. George told me several times that he didn't care for his assistant manager at all and claimed Thomas was clawing his way to the top. Yet, at Carole's party, Wanda said the opposite and made it sound as though George and Thomas were as thick as thieves."

"I visited the bank under the pretense of opening an account and met both of them. You're right about Wanda, and I crossed her off the list. I didn't rule out Thomas, given his past. He's from Chicago and worked at a local bank for four years before coming to California. He was fired from his position for *unknown reasons*. At least, that's what we were told. Son of a gun..." Preston backed away from the microscope and brushed his hand through his hair. "Come here, Vivian. Look at this."

She went over and peered into the microscope. "Is this some sort of joke? It's sodium chloride...table salt. I didn't save your life after all."

"This fella has a sick sense of humor. He could have easily gotten rid of me. Why didn't he?"

Vivian looked into the microscope again. "It seems the game he's playing is more psychological than anything else. So far, he's taken great pleasure in evoking fear into us without imposing any real harm. That movie certainly terrified me."

Preston paced across the room. "That would explain why he displayed the photographs of George and Tilly in her hotel room. He wanted to shock you by finding out about their affair, but he killed Tilly, so it's not all psychological."

"Did he, or are they two separate issues? That's the trouble. All we have are speculations. We don't know if George stole the coins or not. Any one of those six suspects could have taken them, except for Wanda, and Tilly might not be involved in this at all." Vivian walked over to the balcony to check on Bella again. "I still think Captain Kynette killed Tilly on the mayor's orders and tried to frame me for it. If George stole the coins, maybe he confided in someone else entirely."

"Who else would he tell?"

"He had a couple of close friends, one in particular I wouldn't dismiss so easily. The bottom line is, we have a hundred different scenarios without anything concrete."

Preston swore under his breath. "It's Thursday already, and I have until Sunday to find the coins. The attorney needs to notify the family and report the theft to the police on Monday morning. Once it goes public, we'll never find them."

Gunther knocked on the door and opened it just enough to peek inside. "Sir, your parents are home, and your father would like a word with you. He's in the den."

"All right." Preston headed for the door. "This will just take a minute."

After he left, Vivian stayed on the balcony for a while, deep in thought. Finally, she went inside and sat down in the chair behind the desk. She reached over to look through George's file again, but her foot hit something on the floor. Vivian pushed the chair back slightly, bent down, and saw a small box tucked underneath the desk. Using the toe of her shoe, she flicked the top off.

A couple of photos spilled out. She looked closer and her face flushed hot. These were the *items* Preston had found in Tilly's hotel room. Angrily, she grabbed the box and put it on the desk. Right off, she could see the contents of the photographs, and it made her sick. She disregarded them, pulled out one of the letters, and read the first few paragraphs.

Gunther cleared his throat as he stood in the open doorway. "Miss Steele?"

She put the letter down. "Yes?"

"I'm sorry to disturb you. May I speak with you for a moment?" With her nod of approval, he approached her and kept his voice low. "I apologize for overstepping my bounds. We all have our crosses to bear and our secrets to keep, including myself, which is why I never sent my condolences to you after your mother passed away. It broke my heart to hear of your loss. She was a remarkable woman."

Vivian gazed at him curiously for a moment, not knowing how to respond, but then she glanced behind him.

"This is between us, Miss Steele, and no one else," he assured her. "Arthur can attest to my integrity, assuming you keep in touch with him."

Her eyes lit up. "You know Arthur?"

"We were friends years ago. Please, give him my best, and if you ever need anything at all, I am at your service."

She stood up when he turned to leave. "Gunther...thank you."

He smiled at her and headed out the door.

What Gunther told her may have taken her completely by surprise, but it couldn't have been more perfectly timed. She shoved George's letter back into the shoebox, closed the lid tight, and stuck it back under the desk where it belonged. By the time Preston returned, she'd made up her mind.

"I'm going home," she told him.

Preston stopped short. "What's wrong?"

"Nothing. I think we're done here, and I want to go home. Come along, Bella. Let's go." She swept by him determinedly, but he caught her arm.

"What is it, Vivian?"

She lifted her head and looked up at him. "There's no doubt in my mind now that George stole those coins. I'm going home to search for them. They have to be there somewhere."

"What convinced you?"

"I just read George's letter to Tilly about running away together. On the night George died, he said the bank was sending him to Sacramento on a business trip that weekend. He lied, of course. In the very next sentence, he told me that the bank had provided him with a sizeable bonus. *Provided* was a strange word for him to use in that context, don't you think? Most people would have said they received a bonus, or the bank gave them a bonus. Am I looking too deeply into it?"

"First of all, I'm sorry. I should have put that box somewhere else," Preston told her. "In answer to your question, I agree with you. That letter, along with the movie, convinced me that George took the coins. He probably knew he needed a windfall of money to convince Tilly to run away with him, and the only way they could be together was to leave town. You realize they were running away from the mayor, too, but he ended up stopping them."

She hadn't thought of that. "We just narrowed down the possible suspects. I'm going home to look for the coins. I'll let you know if I find anything."

"Whoa, hang on, Vivian. Until you get your locks changed, I'm not letting you go home by yourself."

"Don't be ridiculous." She called to Bella again, and both Bella and Boris joined her as she walked down the stairs. "As you pointed out, I'm carrying a handgun in my purse, and I know how to use it."

"I don't doubt that but let me help you look for the coins. Like it or not, we need to work together on this. Until we find those coins, we don't know what else our mystery man has up his sleeve."

"I'm tired. This can wait until tomorrow."

When they reached the bottom of the stairs, Boris headed down the hallway and Bella went with him. Vivian kept calling Bella, but it fell upon deaf ears. She hurried after them and ended up in the living room. She stopped when she saw a petite older woman standing in the room petting Boris and Bella.

"That's my mother," Preston told her. "I'll introduce you to her."

Vivian went along with him, although it was strange. She knew Preston lived with his parents, and Carole had spoken highly of them, but she never pictured them in her mind. Even if she had, given her dislike for Preston, she would never have imagined his mother appearing so sweet and charming as she turned her smile on them.

"Preston, who do these adorable puppies belong to?" his mother asked, and she noticed Vivian. "Oh, hello, dear."

"I'm Vivian Steele. It's an honor to meet you, Missus Stone."

"Well, aren't you lovely? It's very nice meeting you, Vivian. My son never introduces me to his friends. Are these your pups?"

Vivian couldn't help but smile back at her. "The little one is. Her name is Bella."

"The Saint Bernard is Boris, Mother," Preston said. "I'm watching him for a few hours for another friend."

"I really should get home now. Come along, Bella." But Bella sat down and refused to leave Boris' side. Vivian picked her up. "Thank you for letting us visit. I'll call you tomorrow, Preston. Again, it was nice meeting you, Missus Stone."

"I'll walk you out," Preston said.

Vivian didn't wait for him. She made her way to the front door, walked to the carport, and got into her car. She ignored Preston's protests and drove away. For a while, she thought about the tangled mess that was going on around them, but Gunther entered her mind. She was anxious to talk to Arthur now and find out how the two of them knew each other.

When Vivian was about half a mile away from her boutique, she kept her eyes planted on the lighted road ahead of her, looking for a patrol car in the vicinity. Instead, she spotted Preston leaning against the lamppost in front of her building with his arms folded as though he'd been standing there for hours.

"Oh, good Lord…" She turned into the alley, stopped her car, and got out. "Now I know you're an only child. You just do whatever you want, no matter what other people say. Where did you park your car?"

"It's well hidden. Don't worry."

Vivian shook her head as she opened the side door and turned on the light. "Your mother seems like a darling woman. That took me by surprise."

"I'm sure it did," he chuckled. "You probably envisioned my parents having horns growing out of their heads."

She couldn't help but laugh. "Something like that. This is the back room of the boutique. There's a storage room across the hall with all of George's things."

Preston walked around and looked into the display room. "This is a very elegant shop."

Vivian set her purse on the table and pulled out her sketches from her carry bag on the counter. "These are my drawings from the movie."

He walked over to her. "What does Bella have in her mouth?"

"I don't know." Vivian squatted down. "Come here, Bella."

She pranced over to her with an envelope between her teeth.

Vivian took it from her and saw *Missus George Ramsey* typed on the front. "I don't like the looks of this. Someone must have slipped it under the door. It's from the same person who sent the movie ticket."

"Do you want me to open it?" Preston asked, and she handed it to him. Carefully, he lifted the flap and pulled the note out. "*Griffith Park Observatory. Nine o'clock tomorrow morning. Come alone.*" He flipped it over and gave it back to her. "That's all it says."

Vivian read it. "There's no mention of the coins, but I suppose it's assumed I should bring them with me...if I had them. Preston, did you notice the handwriting on the note?"

He looked over her shoulder. "What about it?"

"A woman wrote this. Most men write with a heavier hand and without swirls and curls. Not only that, but her hand was shaking at the time. See the slight wiggling on the capital letters?" Vivian looked up at him. "Either the woman has some sort of illness that causes tremors, or she was frightened."

18

Hollenbeck Park

"That's the last box." Vivian took another look around the storage room. "The coins aren't here."

"Can you think of any other place George could have put them?" Preston asked.

"No." She wandered into the back room. "I'm worried about tomorrow. What are we going to do? All I can think about is the woman who wrote that letter. What if he intends to hurt her when I don't show up with the coins? We should call the police, but Captain Kynette might be involved."

Instantly, Preston was by her side. "Even if he isn't, that's a bad idea. With two million dollars at stake, I don't trust anyone in the police department. I have a plan."

"Oh, I can't wait to hear this." She sat down at the table, but the telephone rang, and she stared at it. "It's after eleven o'clock. No one calls the shop this late at night."

"It might be Freddie," Preston said. "I left a message for him to call me here when he picked up Boris."

Vivian lifted the receiver. "Hello?" She rolled her eyes and handed the phone to him.

While Preston spoke to Freddie, Vivian slid her writing pad and pencil over and jotted down the names of those possibly involved. She included Captain Kynette, Thomas Goldman, and David Sampson. Another thought struck her, but her ears perked up when she overheard Preston tell Freddie that her boutique would be closed tomorrow.

"No, Vivian will let Nora know," Preston said, looking at her. "Nick is going to help me tomorrow. I don't want too many people around, but I'll call you first thing in the morning and let you know for sure. I'm glad you had a good time with her. Yes, Boris was a perfect gentleman. Good night, Freddie."

Vivian glared at him as he hung up the phone.

"Before you say one word, hear me out..."

"That's not how this works, Preston. I don't know who you're working for or who the hell Freddie is, but don't you dare tell me that he's the man who Nora met at the bus stop this morning."

"It was for her own protection."

Vivian shot to her feet. "You have no right to..."

"Think about it, Vivian! Nora is the closest person to you and works here six days a week. You said yourself that your jacket was stolen right off the rack, which means our mystery man waltzed right into your shop without either of you being the wiser. After watching that movie, I asked Freddie to keep an eye on Nora just to be safe. They're about the same age, and they're getting along rather well. He's being very discreet. She doesn't know anything about what's going on."

Preston succeeded in silencing her. She'd been so focused on herself and George, his death and his infidelity, Tilly's murder, the movie, and now the coins, she selfishly neglected to consider Nora's safety. Her heart started racing with the mere thought of Nora getting hurt because of her. "Thank you..."

"You're welcome."

Vivian sat at the table again and motioned for him to do the same. "I was writing a few names down, and we might have forgotten someone. You said only a handful of people know the coins are missing. Were you including the security guard?"

"What security guard?"

"At the bank, Chester's attorney was undoubtedly escorted by a security guard to the vaulted room where they keep the safety deposit boxes. The guards aren't allowed inside the room, but maybe he stood by the doorway and noticed the coins were gone. It's just a guess."

"The attorney didn't mention anyone else being present, but it's worth checking into. A security guard would also know who had access to the coins." He picked up the phone and dialed a number. "Barney, it's Stone. Sorry to bother you so late, but can you find out the names of the security guards working at Bank of America on Hollywood Boulevard, preferably those who were working last Friday? Yeah, I know. Just see what you can do. Also, I'm going to need Nick's help tomorrow. If you talk to him before I do, let him know. Great, thanks. I'm not home, so call me back at..." He looked at Vivian.

"Brighton four–five thousand. That's my private number upstairs. I need a glass of wine."

"I'll join you." Preston repeated the number to Barney and hung up.

Vivian stared at him for a moment. "Who the heck are you, Preston Stone?"

"I'm wondering the same thing about you."

"As much as it pains me to say, I've changed my mind. If you don't mind sleeping on the couch, I think I'd like some company until I get the locks changed."

"I thought you'd never ask," he laughed. "Let me grab a bag from my car. I'll be right back."

Vivian waited for him to return and led the way upstairs. She poured two glasses of wine and joined Preston in the living room. He was sitting on the couch with Bella curled up and sleeping right beside him.

She sat in the chair. "We need to figure out what we're going to do tomorrow. You mentioned having a plan?"

"It's a rather simple one," he said while gently petting Bella. "There were twenty-five gold and silver coins in the collection, dimes, quarters, and silver dollars, with a total weight of about twenty-five to thirty ounces. All we need to do is fill a pouch with a similar weight in newer coins and try to pass those off to him."

Vivian gave him exactly three seconds to recant his *simple* plan. "Since this lunatic wants me to go to the observatory alone, what should I tell him when he discovers they aren't the coins that he's willing to kill for?"

Preston loosened his tie. "Okay, now you're being unreasonable."

"I tend to be unreasonable when I'm tired, and my life is on the line."

"He's not going to just walk out of the shadows and ask you for the coins," Preston argued. "I guarantee he's going to have someone else pick them up from you, like the blonde-haired, *skinny as a rail waiter* who put the salt in my champagne. Or he'll get a message to you letting you know where to leave them. And you won't be alone. Nick and I will be watching you every step of the way."

She didn't like it one bit, but she couldn't think of a better plan. "Our hands are tied, aren't they? That woman's life is at stake, too. Still, there's so much that could go terribly wrong."

"We don't know if the woman is in trouble. She might be working with him and wrote the note while traveling in a car. Either way, I think we need to give it a shot. It's our best bet for catching this guy, but if you don't want to, I understand. You'll be putting yourself in a great deal of danger, and you're not accustomed to this line of work...are you?"

Vivian knew he was fishing for information and sipped her wine. "I agree we need to go through with this."

"First thing in the morning, we'll go to the bank to get the exact weight of the coins. If Barney comes up with the names of the security guards, I'll have Freddie track them down while we go to the observatory."

"There's a cash register downstairs with plenty of nickels, dimes, and quarters. I also have a small kitchen scale, and I can carry the change in one of my jewelry pouches. I just thought of a little glitch in the security guard theory. As I said, after seeing my drawing, Henry from across the street said the wingtips shoes were custom-made at Robertson's in Malibu. That's a rather high-end shoe store, and I'm not sure a security guard could afford to shop there."

"Did you bring those sketches up here with you?"

Vivian went into the kitchen to fetch her blue carry bag. After she handed Preston the sketches, she pulled out her pad and a charcoal pencil, then she sat down in the chair and started drawing a few other sketches.

Preston flipped through each one. "Vivian, these are excellent. This is exactly what both of the actors looked like, and you captured every detail of the background. You'd make one hell of a great crime scene artist. Hold on..." He set the others aside, leaned forward, and studied one of them.

"What is it?"

"This is the sketch of the woman in the movie before she went into the kitchen. You included the painting hanging on the wall behind her. I've seen it before."

"It was a painting of Hollenbeck Park in Boyle Heights with the brick pathway edging the lake, and the pedestrian bridge in the backdrop. I've been there."

"No, I mean, I've seen this exact painting someplace. It was at someone's house, but I can't remember where." The telephone rang, and Preston looked at her. "That's probably Barney."

"The phone is on the kitchen counter." As Vivian continued working on her new sketches, she remembered going to Hollenbeck Park with George a few times to walk along the path. Once, Becca came with them. They rented a rowboat and had such a fun afternoon.

Thinking about Becca suddenly spurred another memory. After George's funeral, she had given Becca a box of family photographs that George had kept after he and Ruth divorced. It had been tucked in the back corner of their bedroom closet, and she never looked through it before giving it to Becca.

Preston came back into the room. "Barney found out the names of the two security guards who were working when the attorney discovered the coins were missing. Mike Costanza has been at the bank since it opened twenty-four years ago."

"I met Mike and his wife before. It was at a picnic the bank hosted for the employees. He didn't have anything to do with this."

"I agree. I'm crossing him off the list. Jack Farrell, on the other hand, was hired a year ago from an independent security company. He's only twenty-eight years old. I bet he was the guard on duty when I went to the bank to meet with Thomas and Wanda."

"What did he look like?" Vivian asked. As Preston described him, she started sketching the man's face. She asked him more specific questions about the man's eyes, nose, mouth, eyebrows, forehead, etc. When she was done, she showed him the picture.

"Jesus, that looks exactly like him. Who is the man you drew next to him?"

"It's the blonde waiter at Carole's party. I only saw him from a distance, so I couldn't capture all the details of his facial features, but it's a pretty good likeness of his physical stature."

"Do me a favor. Can you draw a picture of Thomas Goldman?"

"I already did." She flipped to another page in the pad and showed him.

"That's terrific. I want to show these to Nick. He'll be at the observatory tomorrow, and these will help us keep our eyes out for some familiar faces."

"I'll draw one of David Sampson, George's best friend, and Captain Kynette, too, just to cover our bases," Vivian said.

"Do you mind if I have another glass of wine?"

"Not at all. Help yourself. The bottle is in the refrigerator. I'll take one, too."

Vivian handed her glass to him and continued sketching. When Preston returned, he set her drink on the table beside her and sat next to Bella again. Vivian concentrated on her drawings, flipped to the next page, and sketched Captain Kynette in the courtroom.

"By the way, I might know where George hid the coins," she said. "The trouble is, the only way to find out is by talking with his ex-wife and asking her if I can look through a box of photographs that I gave to Rebecca, their daughter. I'm sure you're aware that George was married before. It's probably in his file."

"I read about them. Can you talk to Rebecca instead of her mother and ask her if she found any coins?"

"She's visiting Ruth's parents in Arizona, but that's not a bad idea. I have their phone number. There...I'm done." She leaned over and handed him her pad. Then she glanced at the clock. "It's after midnight, and we have a busy day tomorrow. I want to get at least a couple of hours of sleep. You don't have to stay here tonight, Preston. The couch isn't very comfortable. Seeing the woman's handwriting on that note just unnerved me, but I'm okay now."

"I'm not going to argue about it," he told her. "I don't mind sleeping on the couch. Surprisingly, I can sleep anywhere."

She got up and grabbed her handbag off the end table. "That doesn't surprise me one bit. There are extra pillows and blankets in the linen closet next to the bathroom down the hall to your left. Help yourself to more wine. And Preston, my bedroom door will be locked, and I've got my trusted gun with me," she added, patting her purse. "Time for bed, Bella."

19

The Observatory

Friday, May 6

Vivian opened one eye, then the other. A few rays of early morning sunlight streamed through the window and shined on Bella, who was furiously scratching at the bedroom door with both front paws as though determined to dig a hole right through the wooden structure. But it was the smell of strong coffee that felt like a splash of cold water on Vivian's face. She jumped out of bed and threw her bathrobe on.

Preston was in the kitchen. He'd changed into a more casual knit sweater and pants, and he was down on one knee, petting Bella while searching through the lower cupboards.

Vivian leaned against the door, watching him. "What are you looking for?"

"Good morning. You wouldn't happen to have a toaster anywhere, would you? I found a loaf of bread."

"You're going to make breakfast?"

He laughed. "If you like toast, I am. That's the extent of my cooking abilities."

Vivian pulled the Toastmaster out of one of the bottom cupboards, set it on the counter, and poured herself a cup of coffee. "Do you hear that?"

Bella started barking and raced into the living room.

"Someone is knocking on the door downstairs." Vivian went over to the kitchen window. "Rats! Carole's car is parked out front. It's only seven o'clock in the morning. She never stops by this early. It's because I left her party without telling her. Stay here, Preston. I'll try to smooth things over with her as quickly as I can and send her on her way."

She opened the apartment door, and Bella raced down the stairs. Vivian followed along behind her, frantically trying to think of what to say to Carole, and how to get rid of her without her suspecting something was wrong. She unlocked the back door, and Carole pushed her way inside.

"What are you doing here?" Vivian asked.

"I dropped Clark off for an early photo shoot. I tried calling you several times last night, but you didn't answer the phone." She tossed her handbag on the table, pulled a chair out, and sat down. "What the hell is going on, Vivian? And don't tell me nothing. I saw you and Preston talking by the bar yesterday, and the next thing I know, you're driving away. If that big oaf said something to upset you, why didn't you tell me? Clark would have talked to him, and if that didn't work, I would have dragged him out by his ear."

"He's not the reason I left. I didn't feel well and..."

"Oh, don't give me that. You know better than to lie to me. Something must have happened between the two of you. Otherwise, you wouldn't have left without a word." Carole folded her arms. "Now, out with it! I'm not going anywhere until you tell me."

"Vivian!" Preston called from the stairway. "Do you have any cinnamon?"

Carole's mouth dropped open, rendering her speechless, while Vivian's eyes narrowed, knowing Preston had been listening to everything they said and deliberately made his presence known. Unfortunately, Carole recovered from her shock a little too quickly and gave her the once-over from head to toe as Vivian stood there in her bathrobe.

"Carole, it's not what you think!"

Carole ignored her. "Isn't this interesting? It's also a little surprising." She snatched her purse and stood up. "I'll let the two of you get back to...well, whatever it was you were doing. Be careful, Viv. We both know he's a slippery rascal."

Vivian followed her to the door. "You know me, Carole. There is no way in hell anything is going on between us!"

"No? Then what is it?" Carole asked as she tapped her foot impatiently, waiting for an answer.

Vivian felt like an idiot and silently cursed Preston.

Carole winked at her. "Call me later, Viv." And she walked out the door whistling *Cheek to Cheek*, the love song from the musical *Top Hat*.

Vivian slammed the door shut and stormed across the room. "Come on, Bella." She stopped in the hallway when she saw Preston standing on the steps. "The cinnamon is in the top right cupboard next to the sink. You did that on purpose."

"I was afraid you would tell her the truth."

"Shut up and go make your toast." She climbed up the stairs, entered the kitchen behind him, and picked up the telephone. "In case you're wondering, I'm calling Nora to let her know the boutique is closed today. It seems you get your way on all things."

Preston handed her a cup of coffee and a small plate with two slices of cinnamon toast on it. "You're just cranky because you haven't eaten."

Vivian couldn't have sighed any louder if she tried, but the buttery sweet smell of the toast made her mouth water. She picked up a slice and dialed the number. "Good morning, this is Vivian Steele. Is Nora there? Oh, please don't wake her, Nancy. I apologize for calling so early. Could you tell her that the boutique will be closed today, and I'll talk to her later? Yes, I'd like to meet with you about the salesclerk position. Why don't you come by tomorrow morning, and we'll discuss it. You're welcome. I'll see you then."

"Who is Nancy?" Preston asked after she hung up.

"Nora's roommate."

Preston sat down at the table. "After you went to bed last night, I put your sketch of the security guard in my car, then I called Freddie and told him to pick it up. He's going to track him down this morning and follow him. Nick is meeting me in the park near the observatory, and he'll join the other visitors on one of the tours. Every Friday there's both an indoor tour and an outdoor hiking tour scheduled for nine o'clock, making this more difficult, which I'm sure our mystery man is counting on. I'll be somewhere nearby within the trees on the hill surrounding the main building."

"I'm supposed to just walk around aimlessly until he or someone else contacts me? I'm going to feel like a sitting duck."

"I told you, the two of us will be watching you every step of the way. Keep in mind, this guy wants the coins and until he has them in his possession, he's not going to hurt you."

"I hope you're right."

At eight-fifteen, Vivian was dressed and wrote a note to leave on the front door of the boutique, notifying customers the shop was closed. After Vivian left Bella at Maria's next door, she gathered her sketches and the measured pouch of coins. She also made sure her gun was still tucked inside her purse. Preston had parked his Jaguar behind the Post Office, and they took different routes to their destination.

No doubt, Vivian was nervous, although she wouldn't admit it to anyone, least of all Preston. Before moving here, she had dealt with all kinds of people, good, bad, and even wicked, and one thing she learned was that those who behaved erratically, without any apparent rhyme or reason, were far more dangerous than any other type of criminal.

This fella had gone to the extreme of that definition by killing Tilly then leaving the photographs on display in the hotel room, tricking her and Preston into watching a violent movie that depicted their own deaths, and putting grains of salt in Preston's champagne instead of poison. Even the two notes to her were formally addressed to her married name. All of it followed the same type of odd and unpredictable pattern, which is what worried her most.

Vivian took Ferndell Drive and turned onto West Observatory Road, which led directly to the parking lot near the main building. Griffith Observatory was a popular tourist attraction with a beautiful planetarium, one of the largest telescopes on the West Coast, and a variety of space and science-related exhibits. It was also the closest place to view the *Hollywoodland* sign that had been erected on Mount Lee, and there were guided tours for those who wanted to take a two-and-a-half-hour hike to the sign through Beachwood Canyon.

Vivian parked in the small lot that was filling up fast with both cars and tour buses. She sat in her car for a few minutes, staring at the domed observatory and envisioning every possible scenario, preparing herself for anything.

Finally, she opened the car door and slowly walked up the ramp with a small crowd of visitors. She tried to keep her distance from the others as they waited for the observatory to open and wandered around the concrete platform that surrounded the building. Along the way, she took a mental picture of the male visitors who didn't seem to be part of a large group or a family.

Of course, she didn't know what Preston's friend looked like, but if she were to hazard a guess, he was the tall, good-looking blonde wearing a tropical blue and yellow shirt and a pair of sunglasses leaning against the building.

At nine o'clock, two employees opened the front doors of the observatory, and people flooded inside. A third employee carried a sign outside and posted it near the dirt path to Beachwood Canyon. Then he announced the hiking tour would begin in ten minutes and anyone who signed up for it should gather by the path. Several people, dressed more casually, headed over to join him.

As each moment passed, Vivian grew more nervous as she continued her stroll, not knowing what else to do. The anticipation was always the best part or the worst part, depending upon the situation, and if she were truthful, she'd admit that she was crawling out of her skin right now. So, when a whistle blew, she jumped a mile before realizing it was the tour guide alerting everyone that it was time to leave, and a group of about twenty-five hikers walked down the path.

Vivian resumed her nervous trek along the front of the building, but not more than five minutes later, a blood-curdling scream echoed through the canyon, and a whistle started blowing over and over again. Two security guards burst out the front doors, raced across the platform, and down the path.

Vivian hurried after the guards, but when she reached the path, the heels of her shoes stuck in the dirt, nearly throwing her to the ground. After taking them off, she carried them with her and ran barefoot the rest of the way.

The group of hikers were huddled together by the time she caught up to them, and Preston was standing among the group. He spotted her and, while frowning, he tipped his head toward the security guards. She looked over and saw the two of them with the tour guide just off the path in a patch of low brush.

A woman was lying at their feet.

Vivian's heart stopped beating for a second. The woman was wearing a red blazer that was identical to hers. As discreetly as possible, she moved closer for a better look and took in a sharp breath. The woman was the female actress from the movie, and it appeared she'd been dead for at least a couple of days, judging from the distinct marbling appearance of her face. Vivian quickly turned away from the scene.

Preston wandered over to her. "She looks familiar, doesn't she?"

"She's been dead for at least two days. None of this makes any sense. Why kill her and leave her here? For all he knows, I had the coins with me. And she's wearing my red jacket, Preston. It seems like he's targeting me more than you."

"Oh, I think he's targeting both of us, if those buzzards over there are circling something other than an animal carcass. I'm guessing the male actor from the movie met his demise, too."

Vivian followed his gaze. Four or five vultures were flying low around the Hollywoodland sign in the distance. "This lunatic seems more determined to put on a shocking show rather than getting his hands on the coin collection. At the same time, it feels like he's building up to something even bigger, doesn't it?" She suddenly stiffened. "I hear police sirens."

"Okay, that was a little too quick. Either you were right about Kynette's involvement in this or someone else called the police ahead of time. Let's get you and your car out of here. The parking lot is directly behind us through the grove of shrubs."

Vivian quickly slipped her shoes on, and they both disappeared into the brush. "Where's your friend?"

"He went back to his car in Griffith Park after we heard the tour guide start blowing the whistle. At least there's only one road into the observatory and a separate road out."

The two of them reached the parking lot and rushed over to her car. Vivian got into the driver's seat. "Preston…"

"I see it." He picked up the piece of paper on the passenger seat and read it out loud, "*You didn't come alone.* This guy is really grating on my nerves. Let's go."

Vivian started the car and drove down the road exiting the observatory.

20

Two-Toned Wingtips

Vivian pulled into the parking lot on the other side of Griffith Park, and Preston pointed to the white convertible sports car in the shade. The blonde wearing the flashy shirt with palm trees and pineapples was standing beside it. He wandered over after they parked the car.

"What the heck happened back there?" Nick asked.

Preston showed him the note. "He knew what we were up to and turned the tables on us. Sometime during the past couple of days, he killed the actress from the movie and dumped her body on the hiking path. Maybe the male actor, too. Nick, meet Vivian Steele."

He reached over to shake her hand. "Nick Campbell. Sorry we're meeting under these circumstances. Are you okay?"

Vivian nodded. "Yes, thanks for your help. He must have seen us at the boutique last night, Preston, or he saw your car behind the Post Office and knew I wasn't coming here alone. That's the only way he would have had time to leave that poor woman's body here. She must have written the note he slipped under my door yesterday, but it seems strange for him to force her to write it days before he needed it."

"We have to find those coins and lure him out into the open," Nick said. "Without them, there's no telling what he'll do next."

Preston looked at Vivian. "You said the coins might be in a box that you gave to your stepdaughter. Where does George's ex-wife live?"

"On Magnolia Boulevard in Encino. That's the only place I can think of where George might have put them. Preston, I'm pretty sure the woman on the path was wearing my jacket. The police are going to wonder why, especially since it's not an article of clothing that I sell in the boutique."

"They'll have to find you first before they can ask you any questions. We'll go to my parents' estate and put your car in one of the garages. You aren't going back to your apartment, not until we catch this guy. You can stay at the estate until then."

Vivian's blood started churning. She straightened her back and stared at Preston. "Hang on a minute. You might be able to order everyone else around, but I make my own decisions. I am not going to hide away like some helpless damsel in distress."

"That's not what I meant."

"Well, that's how it sounded."

Preston reached up and loosened his tie. "You're being unreasonable again, Vivian. You don't seem to realize how serious the situation is and the danger you're in."

She narrowed her steel-gray eyes. "You don't realize what I'm capable of."

Preston stood firm. "Then why don't you tell me?"

"Whoa, settle down, you two," Nick chuckled as he stepped in between them. "Why don't you both take a step back and a deep breath? I'm sure we can come up with a simple solution that will satisfy everyone."

Preston kept his eyes planted on Vivian. "Like what?"

"I have a spare bedroom," Nick quipped, and they turned their glares on him. "It was just a suggestion."

Nick's humor eased Vivian's expression. "I'm willing to compromise a bit. It's a good idea to tuck my car away somewhere for now. I don't feel like dealing with the police, but I'm going to take an active part in this. I'm not sitting by the poolside waiting for the two of you to figure it all out on your own."

Preston sighed. "I didn't expect you to, Vivian. After we get your car in the garage, we'll drive to Encino to talk to George's ex-wife and stop at that shoe store in Malibu. I just don't think you should go back to your apartment until this is over."

"You forget that I have a business to run, and what if our mystery man leaves me another note, but I'm not there to receive it?"

"I think he'll figure out another way to contact you. At the estate, he won't be able to slip a note under the door, not with the security there."

"If I spend the night, I'll need some clothes and personal items, and someone needs to fetch Bella from next door."

"Who's Bella?" Nick asked.

"My Boston Terrier."

"You can take care of all that later, can't you, Nick?" Preston grinned. "You like dogs, and Bella is tiny compared to Boris. Vivian will make you a list of things that she needs."

Nick frowned. "Wait a minute..."

"Right now, why don't you find out how the police knew there was trouble at the observatory and get ahold of Freddie," Preston instructed. "I want to know where that security guard was this morning. Let's go, Vivian. I'll follow you to the estate." They both got into their cars. "We'll meet you back at my parents' place at three o'clock, Nick!" Preston waved to him and followed Vivian out of the lot, leaving Nick standing there alone.

As a precaution, Vivian took the side roads to Santa Monica, which she was familiar with since Arthur didn't live far from the Stone Estate. And thinking of him, she wished she could talk to him right now. This whole thing was getting way out of hand, and with his experience, he would undoubtedly come up with some better ideas, but she didn't want Preston to know about him. Their main purpose for coming to California was to put the past behind them and, knowing Preston, he wouldn't stop digging into Arthur's background until he found something.

Vivian stopped in front of the estate and waited for Preston to open the garage door. She pulled her car inside, grabbed her purse and carry bag, and followed Preston to his Jaguar. "I like Nick."

He opened the passenger door for her. "Most people do."

"I'm dying to ask how the two of you know each other, but you probably wouldn't tell me."

Preston smirked. "Not unless you're willing to share some information about yourself."

"I thought so." She slid into the seat. "I have no idea how Ruth is going to react when I show up on her doorstep. I'm not her favorite person, and frankly, knowing what I do about George now, I don't blame her. If Becca was home, it would be a lot easier."

"Do you want to check out the shoe store first?"

"If you don't mind. That'll give me some time to gather my nerve."

"Vivian, from what I've seen, you've got more nerve than most men I know."

She laughed. "I'll take that as a compliment."

It was a twenty-minute drive to Malibu along the Santa Monica Bay shoreline. Vivan gazed at the beautiful crystal water for a while. Then she leaned her head back and cleared her mind of every thought so she could just enjoy the breeze and the peace and calmness around them.

Preston stopped at the curb in front of the small shoe store. "How do you want to handle this?"

She glanced over at the window display. "Do you mind if I take the lead?"

"Be my guest."

The bell on the door jingled when they entered, and a young man emerged from the back room to greet them. "Good morning. How can I help you?"

Vivian smiled as she approached him. "I have a rather odd question for you. We were at an outdoor charity event the other day, and I saw a gentleman drop a ring of keys in the grass. He disappeared into the crowd before I could return them. I remembered he was wearing the most exquisite pair of two-toned wingtip shoes, so I made a rough sketch of them, hoping it might help us find him. We just came from Harold's Shoe Store in Beverly Hills, and the owner was sure the shoes were one of your custom designs."

"Sure, let me see your drawing."

She handed it to him. "The poor gentleman must be distraught. There were several keys on the ring. If you could find out his name, we would love to return them to him and ease his mind."

"We keep a record of every sale," the young man told her. "I've got to say, this is a great drawing. Do you mind waiting here for a few minutes? My uncle is in the back room. He owns the store and designs all our custom-made shoes."

Vivian waited until he left and kept her voice low. "The only snag in what I told him is if they want to return the keys to the man themselves instead of giving us his name."

"In that case, let me step in," Preston said. "I thought your story was great."

A middle-aged man wearing a pair of wire-rim spectacles came out of the back room. "Good day to you both! I recognize the wingtip shoes from your drawing. I sold them months ago, but I can't remember the customer's name. Let me look in our files." He set the sketch on the counter and pulled out a small metal box filled with index cards.

Vivian and Preston exchanged a glance while they waited.

"Here it is." He pulled a card out. "Yes, it was last fall on October fourteenth. The gentleman was leaving on vacation for Paris the following week and needed a dressy pair of shoes to take with him. His name is…George Ramsey. He lives on West Boulevard in the city." He handed the card to Vivian. "Did you want us to contact him for you?"

Preston placed a sympathetic hand on Vivian's back, took the card from her, and gave it back to the older man. "No, we'll take care of it. Thank you for your help. Have a good day." He and Vivian walked to the front door, but the owner called out to them.

"One more thing! If you can't get in touch with Mister Ramsey, he came into the store with a friend of his. They both bought shoes that day. I wrote his information at the bottom of the card. His name is David Sampson, and he lives at three fifty-four Venice Boulevard in Arlington Heights."

Preston thanked him again. They walked outside, got into the car, and sat there quietly.

"David knew George was running away with Tilly," Vivian said as she stared straight ahead. "It sounds like he planned on taking the same trip to France, which means George told him that he stole the coins. David might even have them."

"I was thinking the same thing, although if he had the coins, why didn't he take the trip to France without George?"

"Maybe he decided to use the money on something else."

"We need to get a look at his financial records. Let's put our visit with Ruth on hold."

"Thank goodness," Vivian sighed. "I couldn't handle seeing her right now. I'd rather talk to Becca first. Maybe we won't have to go to Ruth's at all."

"There's a little café across the street. Why don't we get a cup of coffee and figure out where to go from here? I'm also going to give Barney a call and see what he can find out about David Sampson."

Vivian agreed, and they walked across the street. "Outside of where he lives, I know David works for Seymour Realty on Vine Street, and he and George have been friends since college. He was also at Perino's with another woman other than his wife on Tuesday night when Carole and I went there."

Preston snickered. "Don't tell me he's the guy who had a drink thrown in his face? I saw the whole thing when I arrived at the restaurant."

"Yes, that was David. I may or may not have instigated that argument."

Preston opened the café door for her. "Sounds like he had it coming to him."

"I'm sure you've had a few drinks thrown at you."

"Too many to count," he laughed.

21

Bullock's

There were only a few customers inside the café, and they sat at a table by the window. "Did you want something to eat?" Preston asked.

"I'm not hungry. I should make a phone call, too. Later this afternoon, I'm supposed to meet someone at Cole's Restaurant. Of course, that's out of the question now."

Preston raised a brow. "Do you have a date?"

"It's none of your business, but he's a wholesale buyer for Bullock's department store. The executives were meeting this morning to look over my portfolio and decide if they wanted to carry my designs in their store. He was going to let me know their decision over drinks. Why is it that when the chance of a lifetime comes along, something always gets in the way of it?"

"Don't be such a pessimist, Vivian. He can let you know their decision over the phone just as easily as he could in person. Let me give Barney a quick call first. I'll just take a cup of coffee if the waitress ever wanders over here."

"Now, who sounds like a pessimist?"

After Vivian ordered their coffee and sat there drinking hers, she thought about George, and what a mess he'd left in her lap. As if his infidelity wasn't enough to contend with, he stole two million dollars worth of coins, caused the deaths of up to four people so far, including himself, and put her and a few others in danger. Whatever happened from here, she prayed Becca would never find out what type of man her father was and the destruction that he'd caused.

Preston slipped into the seat across from her and took a swig of his coffee. "You're not going to believe this. Barney talked to Freddie, and it seems our security guard, Jack Farrell, not only works at the Bank of America, but he also works for a couple of other businesses. Are you ready for this?"

"Just tell me."

"Two days a week, Farrell works as a security guard at the Seymour Realty building on Vine Street."

"That's where David works."

"I think that's a little too coincidental. Remember our speculations about Tilly? Let's replace David in that theory. What if David knew George intended to take the coin collection, and that's why they were preparing for a trip to France? But David thought George died before he had a chance to actually steal them. Then last week, the security guard informed David that the coins were gone. David would immediately assume that you had them."

She thought about it. "I don't know, Preston. It seems a little far-fetched that David and the security guard knew each other, let alone being close enough to discuss stolen coins. Frankly, it wouldn't surprise me one bit if David had the coins and cashed them in, but I can't see him threatening and killing people."

"If David had counted on splitting the two million dollars with George and lost his chance, he probably feels entitled to them now. There's also a chance that all three of them were working together, the security guard included."

"I suppose it's a possibility, but again, all we have are speculations. I'm going to make that phone call." Vivian walked over and dialed Gary's number. She let it ring several times before hanging up. She was aching to know what the executives had decided. Some good news would help make all of this a little more bearable. She sat down at the table again. "There wasn't any answer. Where are we going from here?"

"Let's take a drive to Seymour Realty," Preston said. "I'd like to inquire about David's whereabouts this morning. I'll handle this one by myself since you know him, but I doubt I'll be able to come up with a story that would top the one you told at the shoe store."

They finished their coffee and drove to Vine Street. It was twelve-thirty by the time Preston pulled down the side road next to the building and parked a short distance away. As Vivian waited for Preston in the car, she watched the people walking on the sidewalk and driving by in case she saw David coming or going.

It was only a few minutes when Preston returned. "The receptionist said David was out in the field with clients all morning. She wasn't sure if he was coming back to the office today."

"Since we're in the area, would you mind if we made a quick stop?" Vivian asked. "Bullock's department store isn't far from here on Wilshire Boulevard. Someone there should be able to get a message to Gary, the wholesale buyer. I don't want him waiting for me at Cole's Restaurant later, and I never show up. This is too important to me."

"Sure, I know where it is." Preston pulled away from the curb and headed down Vine Street.

The department store was only a few miles away, and Preston dropped Vivian off at the front entrance. She went through the double doors, walked to the elevators at the back of the store, and looked at the directory plaque on the wall. The administrative offices were on the tenth floor, and she was happy to discover that Gary Rutherford's name was listed among the executives.

Vivian got on the elevator and when the doors opened on the tenth floor, a young woman was sitting behind the receptionist's desk straight ahead. She walked over to her. "Good afternoon, my name is Vivian Steele. I tried to call Mister Rutherford earlier, but there was no answer. I wondered if I could leave a message for him?"

"He just came back from lunch. Let me see if he's available." The woman picked up the phone. "Vivian Steele is here to see you. Yes, sir." She hung up. "You may go right in, Miss Steele. His office is the second door on the left."

Vivian thanked her and walked down the hall. She knocked before opening the door and saw a heavyset, gray-haired man sitting behind the desk. "Oh, I'm sorry. I must have the wrong office. I'm looking for Gary Rutherford."

He stood up, smiling. "As far as I know, that's my name. How can I help you, Miss Steele?"

Vivian's voice caught in her throat. "Are...are you the wholesale buyer for the store?"

"I'm one of them, and a rather good one, in my opinion. Why don't you tell me why you're here, and we'll see if I can help you."

Her breaths came short and quick now, and she stared at the floor, scowling and trying to make sense of this. She didn't know what to do.

"Are you all right, Miss?"

"No, not really. It seems someone played me for a fool. A man impersonating you led me to believe...never mind. I'm sorry for disturbing you." She quickly closed the door behind her and tried to steady herself as she walked down the hall to the elevator.

Once inside, Vivian pressed her back against the wall of the elevator and closed her eyes, feeling like her entire world had been shattered again. She couldn't believe it. The whole thing was a lie. There was never a potential contract with Bullocks or an executive meeting. The man she'd met for lunch and at Carole's party was a damn imposter.

To make matters worse, as the elevator traveled down to the main level, it stopped on every floor along the way and filled up with customers. Claustrophobia had never been an issue for her, but right now, she could barely breathe and felt trapped and was desperate to get away from this crowd, the confines of the elevator, and even this moment in time.

When the elevator doors finally opened on the main floor, she practically pushed her way out and headed down the center aisle to the front door. It occurred to her that the imposter was their mystery man, which meant they at least had a face to put on him now, but that didn't help her shake this sickening feeling of being duped.

Vivian reached the double doors and stood there, looking out the window at Preston sitting in his car out front. Telling him what happened was going to be nearly as painful as the rest.

That's when a brief memory flashed in her mind and gave her an idea. She shoved the door open, went outside, and got into the car. "We need to make one more stop in the city."

"All right. Where are we going?"

"The corner of Alameda and First Street." The minute Vivian spoke, she remembered Preston had seen her talking with Lucky on that same corner last Friday. "Don't even think about asking me why we're going there, Preston. You have your friends, and I have mine. Let's just leave it at that for now." And neither of them said another word the entire way, not until fifteen minutes later when they drove down First Street and approached Alameda Street.

"Do you want me to park somewhere?" Preston asked.

"Pull over in front of Lou's Tavern. It's right on the corner." Vivian took a pen and a small notepad out of her purse. "What is the telephone number at your estate?"

"Vivian, what's going on?"

But she sat there, waiting for his answer until he gave her the number. She wrote it down and got out of the car. "I'll be right back."

The tavern was small, dark, and dingy, and reeked of stale beer and cigar smoke. The patrons inside, sitting at the bar and scattered around at the tables, all set their drinks down to stare at her. With a determined gait, Vivian walked over to the bar and waited for the bartender to notice her, which only took a matter of seconds.

"How can I help you, Miss?"

She reached over and handed the note to him. "Please give this to Lucky and tell him it's extremely important."

"Will do."

Vivian left just as quickly as she came and got back into the car. She sat there quietly for a moment. "He called me on my private number, Preston."

"Who did?"

"The man posing as Gary Rutherford, the wholesale buyer for Bullocks. I should have caught that right away. My apartment number isn't listed in the telephone book, and I've only given it out to a handful of close friends." She turned her head and glared at him. "You called me on it, too, right after we saw that movie at the Liberty Theatre. How did you get the number?"

"Uh...well, my friend Barney has access to all the unlisted..."

"Damn it! I'm smarter than that. I've always spotted errors and red flags like that right away, not days later when it's too late. What the hell is wrong with me?"

"You've been dealing with a lot lately, Vivian."

"That's no excuse. Imagine my surprise when I met the *real* Gary Rutherford upstairs at Bullock's. I went out to lunch with the imposter, and he was at Carole's party, too. I played right into his hand like some dolt. If he's our mystery man, I don't know how he ties into all of this, but it seems more likely than not."

Preston perked up. "So, you know what he looks like?"

"I might be able to do better than that. The friend I met here last Friday saw us together after lunch on Wednesday. He might know the imposter's name. If not, I'll sketch the rat's portrait for you, and you can have your friends try to find him. Can we go back to your estate now? I want to wait for Lucky to call me."

"Lucky?"

"Don't even go there, Preston." Vivian threw herself back against her seat and folded her arms in front of her, but when the car didn't move, she glared at Preston again. "What's the matter?"

"We need those coins. If this imposter is our guy, we don't know anything about him. Even with a name, he's too clever to leave an easy trail, so finding him is going to take time. Our only hope is getting our hands on those coins. Barney is checking into David's financial records in case he's already cashed them. Do you have Becca's phone number with you? If not, I think we need to go to Ruth's and check out that box you gave her."

22

Ruth

Vivian was unable to catch even the smallest break. She used the coins from the pouch she'd taken with her to the observatory to make a long-distance call from the payphone in front of the tavern. but Becca's grandfather answered and said she was out shopping with her grandmother.

"I guess we're going to Encino," Vivian said as she got into Preston's car. "Becca wasn't home."

"I'm sorry, Vivian, but if the coins are in the box, we'll at least have the leverage we need to end this sooner, hopefully without any more bloodshed."

"You're right. What's bothering me is Ruth divorced George three years before I met him. Even so, I'm going to get the sticky feeling she's looking at me like I'm one of the women he was seeing when they were married. Let's just get this over with."

Preston started the car and drove off. The two of them said very little during the half-hour ride to Magnolia Boulevard. After Preston turned onto the road, Vivian pointed to the large ranch made of stucco and fieldstone four houses down.

"Drop me off here, Preston. I'll walk the rest of the way. Then park down the road and watch for me. If she sees me get out of a fancy red Jaguar, it will only instill her already tainted opinion of me."

He pulled over and glanced down at her handbag. "Maybe you should leave your pistol with me. Ruth might give you good reason to use it."

Vivian cracked a smile, but it was short-lived. She took a deep breath, opened the door, and got out. As she walked down the road, she kept her eyes peeled on Ruth's house.

When she reached the long sidewalk that led to the front door, she paused for a minute. Stiff and mechanical, she headed up the cement pathway that was edged with rows of small flowering cactus plants while her mind choked with a hundred different things to say to Ruth...if she answered the door.

Vivian climbed up the steps. She swallowed the lump in her throat and knocked softly. Instantly, the door swung open, and Ruth stood there but said nothing.

"Hello, Ruth."

"What do you want, Vivian?"

She expected a harsh reaction from the woman and her look of disdain, yet it hurt all the more. "I apologize for showing up unannounced, but it's important. I had given Becca...I mean, Rebecca...a box of family photographs that I found in the closet. There might be something of mine inside."

Ruth swung the door open. "I put it in the basement."

"Do you mind if I take a..."

Before she could finish asking the question, Ruth spun around and marched through the living room, muttering, "It's this way."

Vivian caught a frown as she closed the door. Boy, she spotted a red flag right now. Ruth's obvious anger toward her was in direct conflict with her sudden cooperation. Vivian braced herself for the unexpected, if that was even possible. She followed behind Ruth with the dreaded sense that this visit was going to blow up in her face, just like her brief visit to Bullock's.

After they climbed down the cellar stairs, she noticed the storage containers, furniture, lawn tools, and children's toys were all neatly arranged and stacked in an orderly fashion. All except for the lone cardboard box sitting in the corner.

Ruth pointed to it. "Help yourself."

With extreme trepidation and a few uneasy peeks at Ruth, Vivian went over and got on one knee to look through the box. She carefully pulled out framed photographs along with loose packets of photos and set them on the floor. Most of them were pictures of Becca or her and her father, but a few included Ruth.

As Vivian grew closer to the bottom of the box, she noticed Ruth wandering over to an old oak dresser on the other side of the basement. She continued her search, far more swiftly now since she wanted to get the hell out of here, but the second she reached for the last photograph in the box, Vivian snapped her head around.

Ruth stood directly behind her. "Is this what you're looking for?" She held out a single photograph. "It was taken last summer."

Vivian was almost afraid to look at it, and rightly so. It was a picture of George, Tilly, David, and a blonde woman she didn't recognize on a beach in their bathing suits. "Becca didn't see this, did she?"

"No, I went through the box as soon as she brought it home."

Vivian took it from her and stared at it. "It never occurred to me that there might be something inappropriate inside." She stood up. "I'm sorry, Ruth. I should have looked through the box before I gave it to her."

Ruth seemed taken aback by her words. The stern lines on her face eased, and she looked more puzzled than anything else, but she didn't respond.

"Honestly, I just found out about the woman in the picture this past week. I had no idea."

"A leopard doesn't change his spots," Ruth stated. "How did you find out?"

"She called me."

"Oh, my, that took a lot of nerve."

"Ruth, you don't know the half of it. George was up to his neck in trouble, and it all just came crashing down. That's why I'm here. I was looking for something else in that box, but I couldn't find it."

"Did he owe someone a lot of money? Is that the reason he was killed?"

"Why do you ask that?"

"When I finally woke up and realized George was seeing someone else, I hired a private detective to follow him," Ruth told her. "I found out George spent a lot of time at the horse races in Santa Anita Park. I couldn't figure out where he got the money for his secret little pastimes, so I assumed he was using his cash winnings, but we all know gamblers don't always win."

"This just keeps getting better. Our bank records were all in order, too, and I wondered how he managed a secret life. That explains it. In answer to your question, I think his death had more to do with the woman in the photograph than any gambling debt, but I can't be sure."

"What were you looking for in the box?"

Vivian hesitated. "It's best if I don't tell you, at least not right now, but believe me, if at all possible, I'm going to do everything I can to prevent Rebecca from finding out about it."

"She's all I care about," Ruth stated. "It's my turn to apologize to you, Vivian. I showed you that photo on purpose. I didn't think you knew about George's...shall we say, indiscretions? It was a long time ago and even after his death, I guess I can't let go of my resentment toward him. That was a rotten thing to do to you. I'm sorry. Would you have time for a cup of tea?"

"I wish I did, but someone is waiting for me outside."

"Leave everything here. I'll take care of it." Ruth led the way upstairs. "Rebecca will be home on Sunday. Why don't the two of you spend a day together next week? She'd like that."

"I would, too. Thank you, Ruth." After Vivian left and walked to the road, she crumbled the photograph in her hand into a tight ball and stuck it into her handbag. She motioned to Preston, and he pulled the car up.

"Well?" he asked.

Vivian got in. "The coins weren't in the box, but it wasn't a complete waste of time. Ruth and I had an interesting conversation. We'll never be close friends, but we'll get along better now, I think, and I'll be able to see Becca more often, which is important to me."

"That's good, I guess."

"All's not lost. Ruth told me something else about George that I didn't know. He liked to gamble at the racetracks in Santa Anita Park. I'm wondering if that's where he met the man posing as Gary Rutherford. I've never seen him before, so he wasn't a work associate or a close friend."

"Okay, well, that's a start. I'll have Freddie look into it after you sketch a portrait of him."

"Can we go to your estate now? I'm anxious to hear from Lucky."

"Vivian, I've got to ask. How do you know this Lucky fella? His name alone makes me think he's not on the up-and-up."

"I see," she said, nodding her head. "So, everyone named George, Joe, David, and Gary are all straight arrows?"

He chuckled. "Point taken."

23

Missing

As Preston drove to Santa Monica beach, he thought about what Vivian had said at the observatory about their nemesis building up to something bigger. He had the same feeling now. It seemed this guy was deliberately leading them around by the nose, hand-feeding them false clues, teasing them with threats, and dumping a body here and there just to keep them on their toes...and on edge.

The man was in control, and he knew it. He was flagrantly flaunting his superiority, and while overconfidence usually proved to be a criminal's downfall, so far this guy hadn't made one single mistake, at least none that they had noticed. It was only a matter of time before it all exploded, and what worried Preston most was who would be in the crossfire when that happened.

They reached the estate, and he pulled his Jaguar into the carport next to Nick's convertible. He checked his watch. "It's going on three-thirty, so Nick hasn't been here too long. We've got an earful to tell him." Preston walked with Vivian to the front entryway. "I'm starving. What about you?"

"I'm a little hungry now. We haven't eaten since you made cinnamon toast this morning."

"Watch this. I bet Gunther is waiting for us in the foyer. It's like he has some sort of sixth sense. He not only knows the minute someone arrives at the estate, but if my parents or a guest need anything, whether it's a drink, food, or an article of clothing like a sweater, he's right there offering it to them before they even have a chance to ask for it."

"It sounds like he's alert and attentive. There's nothing wrong with that. I thought he was a very nice man."

"He is," Preston said as he opened the door. "I just find it uncanny."

Vivian stepped inside. "It looks like the coast is clear."

Preston glanced around and didn't see anyone. "Huh..."

But the second they walked into the sitting room, Gunther appeared, seemingly out of nowhere. "Good evening, sir. It's nice to see you again, Miss Steele. Nick Campbell is waiting for you on the pool patio. I stocked the liquor cart, and Henrietta set up a buffet of snacks and sandwiches for you in the living room. Did you need anything else?"

Preston grinned at Vivian. "Were there any telephone calls for Miss Steele?"

"No, sir."

"Thank you, Gunther. I think we're all set." As they headed for the living room, Preston whispered, "See?"

Vivian rolled her eyes. "It's uncanny..."

Preston loosened his tie. "Okay, now you're just being sarcastic."

"Have you noticed you always fiddle with your tie whenever you become defensive?"

He scowled at her. "Well, you have a nervous habit, too."

"And what would that be, Preston?"

"Whenever you're deep in thought, you tuck your hair behind your ears."

She laughed and picked up her pace. "You're being childish."

They found Nick standing at the buffet cart in the living room. "Sorry we're late," Preston said. "We've been checking out all kinds of leads since we left Griffth Park."

Nick piled his plate with finger sandwiches, deviled eggs, garlic knots, and meatballs, and sat down in the wingback chair. "I found out the police received an anonymous tip at nine o'clock this morning, telling them that there was a dead body at the observatory. They identified the woman as Priscilla Peachtree, a part-time actress."

"That poor woman," Vivian sighed. "Did they find anyone else?"

"Nope, and so far, your name hasn't come up in any of their reports."

"That's a relief. Preston, where's your telephone? I have another idea on where to find Lucky."

He pointed to it. "On the side table next to the patio door."

Preston put a couple of small sandwiches on his plate and relaxed on the couch. While Vivian made her call, he filled Nick in on the stops they'd made this morning, starting with the shoe store and Sentry Realty, and he finished by explaining Vivian's encounter with the man posing as a wholesale buyer.

"The trouble is, we don't have any idea who he is, or how he could be tied into this. It seems George was also a gambler, so we're thinking maybe the two of them met at the racetrack, but all we're doing is adding more suspects instead of eliminating them."

"We can cross Thomas Goldman off the list," Nick told him. "I found out why he was fired from that bank in Chicago. I guess he got into a big fight with the president of the bank."

"What did they fight about?"

"The president refused to give Goldman his consent to marry his daughter, so the two of them ran away together and came here to California. They've been married ever since."

"It sounds innocent enough, but didn't you say that Betty, the teller you were talking to at the bank, seemed angry when you asked about Goldman?"

"Yeah, but I also discovered that she's Thomas Goldman's sister-in-law. She was probably worried about me asking too many questions. There's nothing else in his file that sets off an alarm. By the way, Barney said you wanted him to keep looking into some guy who lived on Pearl..."

Vivian joined them. "I wasn't able to reach Lucky."

"You'd better help yourself to some food before Nick eats it all," Preston chuckled, and she wandered over to the buffet cart. "When you're done, can you sketch a portrait of the phony Gary Rutherford? Freddie should be here soon. I'm going to send him to Santa Anita Park. I'm sure they get a big crowd at the racetrack on Friday afternoon. Who knows? Maybe someone who works there will recognize him."

"I have my sketchpad with me. It shouldn't take long." Vivian sat on the other side of the couch and took the pad out of her carry bag.

"Excuse me, sir," Gunther stated from the doorway. "You have a visitor."

"Gunther, just tell Freddie to come in."

"It isn't Mister Barcroft, sir. Miss Carole Lombard is in the sitting room and insists upon speaking with you."

Vivian jumped to her feet. "Carole is here?"

Nick's eyes lit up. "The movie actress? Holy crap, I've been dying to meet her! Show her in."

"Wait a minute, Gunther," Preston said as he stood up. "I'll take care of it."

"Preston, what are you going to tell her?" Vivian asked. "I don't want her involved in this. It's too dangerous."

"What's too dangerous?" Carole spouted as she swept past Gunther, entered the room, tossed her purse on the floor, and plopped down in one of the armchairs. "You're right, Vivian. It was ridiculous for me to think there was any love interest between you and Preston. The police paid me a little visit about an hour ago. I drove to the boutique, but your car wasn't there, so I ended up here. Now, which one of you wants to tell me what the hell is going on?"

Nick set his plate of food down on the table and slid to the edge of his seat, thrilled to pieces. "I'm a huge fan of yours, Miss Lombard. My name's Nick Campbell. I've seen every single one of your movies, and they were all terrific."

"Thank you, Nick. It's nice to meet you." She folded her hands in her lap. "I'm waiting for an explanation."

Preston stepped forward. "What did the police want?"

Carole turned her glare on Vivian. "They asked if I knew where they could find my *best friend*, who promised to be honest with me and include me the next time she was involved in something dangerous."

"I'm sorry, Carole," Vivian said. "What did you tell them?"

"I told them the truth. I didn't know where you were."

"Did they mention why they wanted to know?"

"Oh, no, Vivian, you're not going to get any more information out of me until you tell me what is going on."

Nick stood up. "I think we could all use a drink. What can I get everyone?" He waited, but no one said a word, so he went over to the liquor cart. "Okay, that's four glasses of scotch straight up."

Preston wasn't sure how to handle this. They needed to tell Carole something without telling her everything. "All we know is the police found a dead woman on the hiking trail at Griffith Observatory this morning, and she was wearing a jacket with Vivian's boutique emblem sewn on it. Vivian contacted the police and explained that she sold the jacket to a customer a few weeks ago. It's no big deal."

"No big deal, eh?" Carol said as she took the glass of scotch from Nick. "First, there's a dead woman in the hotel, then the two of you spend the night together, and now there's another dead woman? Don't tell me it's not all connected."

Preston looked at Vivian. "She knows we found Tilly in the hotel room?"

"I didn't tell her that you were there."

"Well, now I know," Carole quipped. "I can't believe you didn't mention that before. Why don't you both start telling me the truth?"

Preston shook his head, but Vivian ignored him. "Carole, outside of being a rat, George stole something of great value before he died. If we tell you anything else, then you'll be in danger, too. You shouldn't even be here. You are my best friend, and I don't want anything to happen to you. Please, let us handle this. I'm begging you."

"We've done everything we can to prevent this from going public, Carole," Preston added. "With your celebrity status, you'd not only be drawing attention to it, but it might put both you and Clark in the most danger of all."

It took a long moment for Carole to respond. "All right." She gulped her drink down, got out of her seat, and faced Preston. "Swear to me on your life that you won't let anything happen to Vivian."

He held a smile on her. "She's doing a fine job taking care of herself, but I swear."

Vivian roped her arm around Carole's. "I'll walk you out." And they headed down the hall.

Freddie passed by them as he entered the room. "What's going on?" He took a double take. "Hey, isn't that..."

"Yes, it was Carole Lombard," Preston told him. "She just stopped by for a visit. I need you to do something for me as soon as Vivian gets back."

"Where's Boris?" Nick asked.

Freddie laughed. "That lazy beast refused to get out of bed, so I left him in the hotel room. What do you need me to do, Preston?"

"Vivian is going to sketch someone she met. I want you to take it with you to the Santa Anita Racetrack and ask around to see if anyone recognizes him. He may or may not be our guy."

"That's terrific," Freddie laughed. "Can I place a bet while I'm there? I've got a five-spot burning a hole in my pocket, and there's a horse named Karloff in the fifth race that's thirty-to-one. Get it. Boris Karloff? I've got a good feeling about it."

"As long as you get the job done as quickly as possible, Freddie."

When Vivian returned, Preston introduced her to Freddie and asked her to draw the portrait. It only took her a few minutes, and when she was done, she showed it to them. "He's in his early thirties and about six feet tall, with hazel eyes and dark hair."

Preston took the sketch from her. "Excellent..." He showed it to Nick, then he gave it to Freddie. "Vivian is waiting to hear from someone who might know his name, so keep in touch, and give me a call if you find out anything."

Freddie agreed. "Sure. What are you and Nick going to do next?"

"We haven't figured that out, Freddie."

"All righty then. I'll talk to you later. Nice meeting you, Miss Steele."

Preston wandered over and sat on the couch. "Are you okay, Vivian?"

"Thank you for helping me keep Carole out of this. I told her that I'd be staying here at least for the night. Can someone pick up Bella for me? Maria has been watching her all day, and I miss her. I also have a travel bag in my closet that should have everything I need inside."

"Leave it to me," Nick told her. "I just need directions to your place, and the keys to get into your apartment."

She told him how to get to her boutique and handed him the keys. "Bella is staying next door at Martino's Delicatessen. Use the side door in the alley to get inside my building. Walk straight through the back room to the hallway and take the stairs up to my apartment. My travel bag is right inside my bedroom closet. I'll call Maria and let her know you'll be picking her up." She went over to the telephone.

"Thanks, Nick," Preston said.

"You owe me," Nick chuckled. "Bella won't bite my hand off or anything, will she?"

He laughed. "She's not much bigger than your hand."

"Oh, I wanted to tell you earlier that Barney found out that guy who lives on Pearl Street moved here from New York City."

"Arthur Romano?"

"Yeah, I guess he retired after thirty years working as a…"

Preston threw his hand in the air, stopping him. "Hang on a minute, Nick." He noticed Vivian looked upset and listened to her conversation.

"Noon? That was hours ago, Maria," Vivian said. "No, that's okay. I'm sure we just got our signals crossed. I'll get in touch with her."

As soon as she hung up, Preston asked, "What's wrong, Vivian?"

"I'm not sure. Maria said Nora came by at noon today and took Bella with her."

"Took her where?"

"I don't know." Vivian picked up the phone again. "I'm going to call the boutique. Maybe Nora didn't get my message this morning and showed up for work." Vivian stood there for a moment, then she held the phone out in front of her and stared at it. "There's no answer."

24

The Photograph

Vivian slammed the phone down. "No one is answering at Nora's, either. Something is wrong. I'm going back to my apartment, Preston. I need to find Bella."

"If Nora is with her, I'm sure she's fine."

"It's not like Nora to go off on her own and pick Bella up like that, and how did she know Bella was at Maria's and not with me?" Vivian grabbed her purse and carry bag.

"All right, but we're going with you," Preston said. "Let's take your car, Nick. It'll be less conspicuous in case the police are watching her building."

Vivian led the way to the carport. Without a word, she opened the passenger door and waited for Preston to get into the back seat.

He looked at her like she had three heads. "Even if I could squeeze back there, you'd need a mammoth shoehorn to get me out."

She folded her arms in front of her. "Well, I'm not sitting back there."

Nick waited in the driver's seat, impatiently strumming his fingers on the steering wheel. "Will the two of you give it a rest? There's plenty of room for all of us in the front seat."

Vivian finally got inside, but with both Preston and Nick standing over six feet tall and well-built, she was cramped and shoulder-to-shoulder with the two of them. So, after Nick headed down the road, she kept nudging Preston's arm over to give herself more room the entire way.

When they reached the boutique, Vivian told Nick to park in the alley. Preston objected, but Nick pulled into the alley anyway and handed Vivian the keys to her building. She collected her bags and hurried to the side door, but it was already unlocked. Thinking Nora was here, she pushed the door open and went inside.

Nick was right behind her. "Holy crap…"

Preston joined them and ran his hand through his hair. "What the hell…"

Vivian stood there in shock. The entire back room was a disaster, as though a cyclone had hit. All the furniture had been tipped over. Rolls of fabric, sewing equipment, tools, and papers covered the floor in a haphazard mess. Vivian rushed into the display room and caught herself at the doorway. Every shelf and rack of clothing had been emptied, with dresses, blouses, skirts, sweaters, and lingerie spread across the floor.

Practically in tears, she ran through the back room to the hallway, passed by the storage room, and raced up the stairs.

"Vivian, wait!" Preston shouted. "The person might still be here."

She ignored him and saw her apartment door was wide open. "Bella!" she cried out as she stepped inside. Like downstairs, the place was in shambles, so much so, she could barely walk into the living room.

Preston joined her. "Our mystery man was here looking for the coins."

"I realize that!" Vivian set her bags down and picked up a few books off the floor, along with nicknacks, pieces of a broken vase, and some loose papers as she slowly made a path to the kitchen. "It'll take me a while, but I can clean up this mess. I want to know where Nora and Bella are."

Both Preston and Nick helped her. "Let's not jump to conclusions," Preston said. "You and Nora seem pretty close. She probably got your message this morning and stopped by around noon to make sure you were all right. If she saw the mess downstairs, she might have called the police, and that's why they were looking for you at Carole's. They probably asked Nora who your closest friends were."

"If that were the case, Maria would have seen the police here and told me about it."

"That's true."

"Maybe this guy showed up after Nora left," Nick suggested.

Vivian stood there, thinking about it. "Nora is a bit of a worrywart. It's certainly possible that she was concerned and came by to check on me, especially since I've been acting strangely all week. She also knows I leave Bella with Maria once in a while, but that doesn't explain why she would take Bella with her." All the blood suddenly drained from her face. "It took hours for someone to do this much damage. What if Nora came here and caught him in the act?"

"Was anyone with Nora when she picked Bella up?" Nick asked.

"Maria didn't say. I just assumed she was alone."

"Why don't I go next door and ask her?" he suggested. "If Nora was alone, there's probably nothing to worry about."

"Be careful what you tell her, Nick," Preston said.

"Don't worry about it. I'll be right back."

Vivian watched him leave. "Preston, I don't care about the coins anymore. I'm worried about Nora. We need to call the police."

"And tell them what, Vivian? The first thing they'll ask you about is the red jacket on the dead woman. You might be able to get away with saying you sold it to her weeks ago, but how are you going to explain why someone ransacked your home and business? Are you going to tell them your husband stole a coin collection worth two million dollars, and someone was here looking for them?"

She glared at him. "Sometimes, I really hate you."

"No, you don't, Vivian. You hate the situation, and I don't blame you. The trouble is, I don't trust the police, and you shouldn't either. Don't forget that you're not one of Joe Shaw and Captain Kynette's favorite people right now. They'd like nothing better than to charge you with...well, just about any crime simply to get you out of their hair. Let's wait and see what Nick finds out at Maria's before we think the worst, okay?"

The telephone rang. "Maybe that's Nora." Vivian carefully stepped over the items on the floor and grabbed the phone. "Hello? Oh, Lucky...I was hoping you'd call. I have a quick question for you. On Wednesday, I think you saw me leave Brookdale Cafeteria with a gentleman around lunchtime. I thought he was a potential client, but since then, I discovered he gave me a false name. You wouldn't happen to know who he Is, would you?"

Vivian listened closely as Lucky explained the man's name was Rocco Rizzoli, a second-rate hoodlum who did odd jobs for a price. He told her that he wondered what she was doing with him, so he did some digging and found out that Joey Carnival had hired Rocco to keep a close eye on her. Lucky wanted to warn her about it, but he couldn't get in touch with her.

"I had no idea. Thank you, Lucky. I appreciate it." Vivian hung up yet didn't move a muscle. Now, on top of everything else, she needed to worry about some lying crook trailing her. Of course, it was her own fault for making a pact with the devil. One thing was for sure. Rocco had nothing to do with the coins.

"Did he give you the imposter's name?" Preston asked.

"Yes, but he doesn't have anything to do with this..." She glanced around the kitchen. Every drawer and cupboard had been emptied with pots, pans, silverware, coffee cups, and glasses dumped on the counter and floor.

"How do you know he isn't involved? What's his name?"

"It doesn't matter, Preston," she said as she shoved some cooking utensils back into one of the drawers. "I'm telling you. He's not involved. You're just going to have to trust me."

"Trust is a two-way street."

"And there lies the problem," she replied flatly.

Nick returned and joined them. "Maria said Nora was alone when she came by, and she was taking Bella to the park. Has Nora ever done that before?"

"A few times, but only after talking to me about it first," Vivian said. "Beverly Gardens Park is just up the road from here."

"There you go," Preston said. "What did you tell Maria, Nick?"

"I lied and said I was Vivian's brother, and we were having a hard time finding Nora. Pretty clever, huh? Sounds like Nora and Bella are okay."

"I hope so, but that was five hours ago." Vivian looked around the kitchen again. She wasn't up to tackling this mess, so she wandered back into the living room. She grabbed the three large cushions and set them on the couch. Then she opened the end table drawer and began putting the contents back inside, which were in a disheveled pile on the floor at her feet.

She spotted her wedding photograph. It took her a moment, but she picked it up and gazed at it for a few minutes. "Arthur was right, George," she whispered, not realizing Preston and Nick had followed her into the room. "This is all your fault."

Preston stepped forward. "Who's Arthur?"

Vivian looked up at him. "Nobody." Angrily, she tossed the photograph back into the drawer.

It made a clinking noise.

They both stared at it. "Preston?"

"I heard it." He reached inside the drawer, pulled the photo out, and gently shook the brass frame. It jingled like a tin can full of coins.

"Well, bust my chops, we hit the jackpot!" Nick exclaimed.

"You and your nephew need to read a different book," Preston snarled at him.

Vivian snatched the picture from Preston, laid it on top of the end table face-down, and carefully tore away at the paper backing. Two dozen silver and gold coins spilled out.

She fell back onto the couch in disbelief. "All this time, they were right here. I was sure George stole them, but I guess deep down, I was hoping I was wrong."

Preston picked up a few to study them. "These are genuine."

"What now, Preston?" Nick asked.

"This puts our mystery man out of commission. Now that we have the coins, he doesn't have a leg to stand on, but we need to find him, whoever he is. He murdered the woman at the observatory, and possibly Tilly. I think Vivian knows who he is."

She stood up. "Let it go, Preston. The imposter isn't our mystery man. He had a completely unrelated reason for tricking me."

"Like what?"

She headed out of the room. "There's probably a jewelry pouch lying around here somewhere for your *precious* coins. I'm going to call Nora and see if she's home now." Vivian went into the kitchen, grabbed the phone, and dialed the number. "Hello, Nancy, it's Vivian Steele again. Is Nora there? What do you mean, she never came home last night? But you said…no, I don't know where she is. That's why I'm calling. When was the last time you saw her? All right, I'll let you know if I hear from her." She hung up. "Preston!"

He and Nick rushed into the kitchen.

"Nancy thought Nora was sleeping this morning when I called, but when Nancy checked on her, Nora wasn't in her bedroom. She's convinced Nora never came home last night. She hasn't seen Nora since yesterday morning."

"Nora worked at the boutique yesterday, didn't she?" Preston asked.

"Yes, but I decided to close early to go to Carole's. Wait, Nora told me that she was going to Ocean Park Beach to see the Kenny Baker concert after work. She was going there with…"

"Damn it!" Preston swore. "Vivian, where are your sketches?"

"By the front door." She and Nick followed him into the other room and watched him rummage through her carry bag.

Preston pulled out one of the drawings and studied it. "I know where I saw this painting before, the one of Hollenbeck Park from the movie." He showed them the sketch. "It was hanging on the wall in Freddie's motel room."

25

Sunset Strip

Vivian chased Preston into the kitchen. "Are you saying Freddie was behind this the entire time? But he's a friend of yours! I don't believe this. He knows everything. I've heard you talking to him on the phone. He knows all about the coins, the suspects, and every single move we've made. How could you let this happen? You had him follow me and even pushed him into meeting Nora..." Vivian's eyes widened in horror. "He has Nora and Bella, doesn't he?"

Preston refused to look at her and went over to the kitchen counter. "I don't know." He grabbed the telephone receiver, but he slammed it back down again. Then he picked up the telephone base and looked at the bottom of it. "That bastard!" Preston yanked a wire out of it. "Nick! Freddie wiretapped her phone and probably mine, too."

Nick stood behind Vivian and placed a comforting hand on her shoulder. "This is crazy, Preston! Freddie is a little on the quirky side, but he's just a rookie. He's only been working for us for a year. There's no way in hell he's involved! He's not capable of pulling off anything of this magnitude."

"We taught him everything he knows, so don't underestimate him," Preston shot back. "He's been hellbent on proving himself. What better way to do it than by beating us at our own game?"

Vivian pulled away from Nick and glared at both of them. "What do you mean, he's working for you?" Preston ignored her and started dialing the phone. She stormed over and pushed the switch hook down, ending his call. "Don't you dare ignore me! I want to know who you are, all of you! I need to know everything about this Freddie character. I don't trust you to find him before Nora gets hurt...if he hasn't hurt her already."

Preston took a deep breath while clenching his fists. "We'll find him. I swear to God, we'll find him, Vivian. Let me call Barney, then we're heading straight to Freddie's motel. He'll be lucky if I don't break his neck. I know this is my fault. It was stupid of me not to look in my own backyard for the bastard."

His words silenced her. So, too, did the outrage in his dark brown eyes as he spoke. Preston had just been double-crossed by someone he'd trusted, and she knew exactly how that felt. "I'm going with you."

He nodded and picked up the phone. "Barney, it's Stone. I want everything we have on Fredrick Barcroft. Yes, Freddie! I want his entire file and every damn piece of information we have on him, no matter how small. Meet us at the Sunset Motel as soon as you can. Look for Nick's car parked next door, and Barney, bring your gun. I'll tell you why when you get there." He slammed the phone down. "Let's go."

"What about the coins?" Vivian asked.

"Put them in your purse in case we need them. Make sure you have your gun with you, too."

"I'll get the coins." She hurried into her bedroom and found an empty velvet pouch on the floor, lying next to a small pile of costume jewelry that had been dumped out. Then she hurried into the living room, gathered the coins, and put the pouch in her purse with her handgun.

Preston and Nick waited for her by the door, and the three of them flew down the stairs. When they reached the alley, Preston insisted on driving. Nick handed him the keys and, again, Vivian was wedged between them in the front seat, but this time she remained silent, worrying about Nora. She would never, ever forgive herself if anything happened to her.

Freddie was a murderer. He had killed both Tilly Trimble and the actress from the movie, and if he was determined to prove himself, as Preston had said, there was no telling what he would do to Nora. The thought that he had Nora in custody since yesterday afternoon upset her even more.

Whereas Preston had taken the blame for not realizing Freddie's involvement, she blamed herself for not protecting Nora from the start when she was hunting for Elliott Kimball. She should have considered the fact that Nora was the closest person to her and in the most vulnerable position should someone seek retaliation against her.

On top of that, she was terribly worried about Bella, too, but the fact that Freddie had a canine companion soothed her a little. Years ago, she'd run across a few criminals who valued and even worshipped their pets, and she hoped Freddie felt the same.

She suddenly snapped her head up with another thought. "The actress didn't write that note."

Nick leaned closer to her. "What did you say?"

Vivian looked at Preston with tears welling in her eyes. "Freddie forced Nora to write that note telling me to meet him at the observatory. I should have known it was her handwriting, but she must have been shaking like a leaf as she wrote it."

It took a moment for him to speak. "Vivian, Freddie viewed both Tilly Trimble and Priscilla Peachtree as expendable. He knew he needed better leverage, something far more personal if he was going to convince you to give him the coins. That's why he's using Nora now. Until he has those coins in his possession, he won't hurt her."

Vivian continued staring at him, trying to figure out from his facial expression if he was stating a fact or simply trying to pacify her.

Preston slowed the car down. "The motel is just up ahead. He's in room Sixteen. It looks like there's only a few cars out front. I don't see Freddie's truck, but let's check his room, anyway." Preston turned into the parking lot at the hot dog stand next door, and as soon as he stopped, another car pulled into the lot.

"Barney is here," Nick announced.

"Tell him what's going on while we head over to the motel. You're coming, aren't you, Vivian?"

"Yes." She took her pistol out of her purse, stuck it into her skirt pocket, and stuffed her purse under the front seat. "I'll leave the coins in the car for now."

Nick quickly introduced Vivian to Barney, then she and Preston led the way to the motel. Nonchalantly, they walked across the parking lots to the end of the motel. Vivian noticed the last room number was Thirty-Two, so Freddie's room was dead center. She counted six cars parked in front of the motel with a large space in the middle, and she hoped this wasn't a waste of time.

As they approached room number Sixteen, they could hear music coming from the open window. Preston motioned for her and Barney to stay on one side of the room while he and Nick passed by the window to the other side. Preston chanced taking a quick peek into the window and nodded to them, letting them know someone was in the room. He and Nick whispered to one another, then Nick walked up to the door.

He pounded on it. "Police! The place is surrounded! Come out with your hands up!"

"What the hell are you doing?" Preston barked at him.

"Where's he going?" Nick said, shrugging his shoulders. "There's only one way out of his room."

Preston nudged Nick aside and kicked the door open. All four of them charged into the room just as the bathroom door shut. The others followed him and tried to open the door while Vivian wandered around, inspecting the room.

The first thing she spotted was the painting of Hollenbeck Park hanging on the wall. Directly underneath it, she saw Nora's colorful beaded handbag lying on the nightstand. Her hand trembled as she picked it up.

"It's not Freddie, but the man went out the window," Preston told her.

Vivian followed them out the door and along the front of the motel. When they reached the end, they saw the man running behind the hot dog stand to the next road over. "Preston, give me the car keys!"

He tossed them to her, and he and Nick raced after him.

"Barney, follow me," she said, and they ran across the parking lot.

Vivian got into Nick's car, started it up, shoved the shifter into first gear, and sped down the road. At the intersection, she ignored the red light, downshifted, and turned right. She had no idea if Barney was behind her or not as she made the next turn, but up ahead, she saw the man they were after hopping into a blue Chevy parked at the curb, and he drove off.

Preston and Nick waited for her by the road. She slowed down, and they got into the car. "Go!" Preston yelled before he even shut the door.

Vivian kept her eyes glued on the Chevy and skillfully weaved around traffic as she shortened the distance between them. She was familiar with many roads in the city and the outlying suburbs since she delivered orders to customers living in pretty much every area and neighborhood.

They traveled west until they crossed the Los Angeles River. The man made a left, heading north to Glendale. Eight minutes later, he turned right, and Vivian stayed hot on his trail for another five minutes.

"He's heading for the Colorado Street Bridge," she said. "I know a shortcut." And she turned off the main road.

"Where are you going?" Preston asked.

"Trust me." She gripped the steering wheel tighter and zigzagged through several rural streets, barely slowing down with each turn.

"You lost him, Vivian," Preston grumbled.

Nick smirked. "No, she didn't. There he is!" He pointed to the blue Chevy that was approaching the bridge from the west while they were traveling to the bridge from the south. "Are we going to hit him?"

"No, but brace yourselves." She didn't lose sight of the car as they closed in on him a quarter mile away from the bridge. She even adjusted her speed to make sure their cars would reach it at the exact same time.

Ten seconds before the two cars collided, the man in the Chevy noticed them and panicked. That's when Vivian slammed on the brakes, throwing all three of them forward, and they watched the man lose control of his car as he passed by them. The Chevy swerved into the other lane and back again with the wheels nearly lifting off the ground before it slammed head-on into the guardrail on the bridge. Thankfully, there were no other cars around. Preston and Nick got out of the car and ran toward the Chevy. Vivian pulled the keys from the ignition and proudly followed along.

The man saw them coming and gathered his wits. He jumped out of the car and started running across the bridge, but Nick easily caught up to him and tackled him to the ground.

By the time Vivian joined them, Preston and Nick had grabbed the man by his arms, lifted him to his feet, and took him over to the side of the bridge. There, they threatened to throw him over the railing into the Arroyo Seco, a very shallow river that was fifteen hundred feet below them.

Preston kept a tight grip on him. "He's the actor from the movie, Vivian."

She walked over and snatched the man by the chin, digging her nails into his skin as she got a good look at him. "Put a blonde wig on him, and he's identical to the waiter at Carole's party. I found Nora's handbag in the motel room. I say, toss him over the railing." She was bluffing, of course, and she hoped Preston and Nick knew that.

But the man started spilling his guts. He rattled on, telling them that his mother was sick and needed an expensive operation, so when Freddie offered to give him ten thousand dollars, he agreed to help him. The trouble was, the man's story went on and on for so long, by the time he finished he said it was his sister who needed the operation.

"This guy is feeding us a bunch of baloney!" Nick yelled. "Let's push him into the river." He and Preston lifted the man by his arms and legs until he was bent at the waist and hanging over the metal railing.

"Okay, okay, I'll tell you the truth!" the man shouted.

They held him there, waiting. "Out with it!" Preston told him.

"I'm Freddie's cousin. My name is Carl Barcroft. Freddie called me and told me about the coin collection and promised to split the money with me if I helped him. I thought we were going to steal it from some rich fella. I had no idea Freddie had concocted such an outrageous scheme. I didn't have anything to do with killing that woman. I swear it!"

Vivian stepped forward again. "What woman?"

"Priscilla, the actress."

"What about Nora?" Vivian asked. "Where is she?"

"The young woman with the little dog? Freddie's got them locked up at the studio. He said we needed them to get the coins."

Preston started pushing him further over the edge. "What studio?"

"It's on Shepherd Drive over in Rose Hills east of the city," Carl said quickly. "It's a private studio in an abandoned warehouse that you can rent by the month. That's where we made the movie."

Preston pulled Carl down off the railing but kept a firm grip of him. "We'll let Barney deal with this guy when he gets here."

"Speak of the devil," Nick said. "Here he is now."

Barney parked before the bridge and walked around the back end of the Chevy. "Cripes, I had a heck of a time trying to follow you. Why doesn't anyone use their turn signals during a high-speed chase? I see you caught the guy. His car took a bit of a beating."

"He's Freddie's cousin," Nick told him. "Did you read anything about him in the files?"

"I flipped through them quickly after Preston called. Let me guess. Is his name Carl?"

"Yep."

"Well, guess what? This young buck must have escaped from the Mack Alford Correctional Center in McAlester, Oklahoma. He's supposed to be serving a five-year sentence for grand theft. I wonder if anyone noticed he's gone."

"Why didn't we hear anything about him," Preston said.

"His notes state Freddie was grilled about his entire family when he signed on, and he was upfront about his cousin's criminal record. They probably didn't think it would pose a problem. It only earned about two brief sentences in his files."

"It *did* pose a problem." Preston looked at Carl. "You're going to enjoy fifteen to twenty years added to your sentence when you return to your prison cell. Barney, get him out of here before the police arrive. We need to find that studio."

Curiously, Vivian watched Barney grab a pair of handcuffs from his car, secure Carl in them, and lead him away. She'd been listening intently to everything they said and had a dozen questions, but right now, Nora took precedence. "Barney, wait a minute!"

"What's wrong," Preston asked.

"We're not thinking this through," she told them. "We can't go to the studio and expect Freddie to just give up without a fight. Even if you offer him the coins, he'll know that his cousin told us where he's hiding, and you have him in custody. We may need Freddie's cousin to barter for Nora and Bella."

26

Payback

Nora sat on the floor in the corner of the dimly lit storage room. Her ankles were bound with a thick rope, and her right wrist was handcuffed to the base of a heavy metal stage lift beside her. Nervously, she kept petting Bella, sleeping in her lap, and she could see poor Boris chained in the adjoining room. He kept staring at her with his big, sad brown eyes.

"It's okay, Boris," she whispered softly, not wanting to wake Bella up. "Everything will be all right, buddy."

Tears streamed down Nora's cheeks again. This was her own fault. She had always shown more caution when she first met someone. Not once had she ever gotten into a car with someone that she'd talked to for only a few minutes. For heaven's sake, how many times had she read in the newspaper about women being attacked or killed by men who they met at a nightclub or on the bus? Outside of that, she and her friends had discussed the dangers and yet, she'd ignored all of it.

Of course, when Freddie wandered by the bus stop yesterday morning and started talking to her, he not only made her laugh, but he pointed to Boris sitting in his truck, waiting for him. Nora loved animals and right off, she fell in love with Boris. She supposed he was the reason that she'd pegged Freddie as a good guy. Stupidly, she didn't think anyone who had such a loveable companion could be a bad person.

It certainly didn't help that Freddie had invited her to hear Kenny Baker sing at Ocean Beach Park yesterday. She'd waited so long for the opportunity to see her favorite performer and couldn't say no. After they got to the beach, they had so much fun, laughing, singing, and dancing in the sand. She was on cloud nine the entire time.

Then, as Freddie drove her back to her apartment, he told her that something was wrong with his truck, and he pulled over to the side of the road. That's when Freddie changed. In the blink of an eye, he turned evil. He was suddenly attacking her, catching her completely off guard, and even though she tried to fight against him, he seemed to have the strength of ten men. He tied her up with a rope, stuffed a cloth in her mouth, and drove off.

The next thing she knew, he was dragging her inside this warehouse.

She'd spent the night and morning right here in this room, and if all that wasn't bad enough, it nearly ripped her heart out when Freddie ordered her to fetch Bella from Maria Martino's earlier this afternoon. She frantically tried to think of a way out of it, but Freddie not only threatened to kill her if she didn't comply, but he described in detail how he would also kill Maria and anyone else inside the shop. She believed him. His black eyes caught a vacant stare as he spoke, as though he was envisioning the act of killing everyone.

Nora nearly burst out crying again, thinking about it, so she leaned her head back against the wall and tried to block everything out of her mind. A second later, she jerked her head up. She heard Freddie whistling as he climbed up the stairs. Bella heard him, too, and lifted her head, and Boris started growling.

As soon as Freddie stuck the key into the lock on the door, Bella jumped off her lap and barked wildly, which set off Boris in the next room.

"Bella, get back here!" Nora shouted above the commotion. "Please, Bella, come here right now."

As soon as the door swung open, Bella raced back to Nora, and she held onto Bella tightly with her left arm. Boris continued barking and howling, and he was on his feet, furiously yanking on his chains, trying to get free.

Freddie scowled at them when he entered the room and slowly approached Nora. "It's time to make our movie."

"I don't understand, Freddie. Why are you doing this?" Nora cried. "I beg you. Let us go. I promise I won't tell anyone. Please, just let us go."

"Don't worry, Nora, as soon as your boss gives me what I want, you can go home." He unlocked the handcuffs and started untying the rope around her ankles, but Boris was making quite a ruckus in the other room. "Shut up, Boris!" Freddie shouted, and he turned to Nora again. "If that damn dog doesn't stop barking, I'll shoot him right where he stands." After Freddie finished untying her, just like that, he was smiling and helping her to her feet. "I won't hurt you if you follow my instructions. We're going to make a quick one-minute film and have dinner together."

Bella growled at him again, so Nora quickly picked her up and held her close to keep her quiet. "What kind of film?"

"Follow me downstairs, and I'll show you. I can't think with that beast barking like a maniac in the other room." He walked out the door, and they climbed down the steps. "All you have to do is sit in a chair with the little mutt, Nora, and read from the script I wrote. Simple, right?"

She fell silent as they made their way over to the makeshift stage. She was practically clinging to Bella now, trying to stop herself from shivering with fear.

Freddie led her over to the single chair propped in the middle of the stage. "All right, sit down here and keep the dog in your lap." He grabbed a piece of paper from the table offstage and handed it to her. "Here's your script. Just read it word for word, nice and slow to make sure your viewer can hear it. I'll be right behind the camera over there the entire time, and I'll cue you when to begin reading. Give me a minute to get everything set up."

She took the paper from him and sat down with Bella.

"You work for a big-shot fashion designer," Freddie said as he turned up the lighting on the stage. Then he adjusted the standing microphone beside Nora. "Don't you get sick and tired of being ordered around and expected to do whatever you're told instead of making your own decisions? I've had a lot of good ideas, but every one of them has been shot down and stomped on. I bet you're a talented fashion designer yourself, aren't you? Has your boss ever once asked you for your opinion?"

Nora was afraid to respond, and thankfully, he let it go.

"I didn't plan on doing any of this, you know," he went on. "Stone pushed me into it. I came from a small town in Oklahoma and spent my whole life listening to the townsfolk talk about what a worthless bum I was, and how I'd never make anything of myself. I finally left, determined to prove them wrong. Where did you grow up, Nora?"

"In Los Angeles..."

"A city girl, eh? Well, it took a lot of hard work and sweat for me to get this job, and I'm damn good at it, way better than that pretty boy Nick by far and a heck of a lot smarter. But no matter what I do, Stone, the filthy rich bastard, keeps treating me like some dumb twelve-year-old kid. By now, I should be in charge of my own team. I finally realized that would never happen, so I showed them. While Stone and Nick are scrambling around like idiots trying to figure out how to stop the *mastermind* behind this scheme, I've been in the driver's seat, dictating to them what to do next, and boy, let me tell you, it feels great."

Nora looked at the script. "I don't understand. This mentions a coin collection?"

"I'm glad you asked. Vivian Steele, your hot-shot boss, is no better than I am, either. Before her husband died, he stole a rich old man's coin collection worth two million dollars. She's been sitting on it ever since, waiting for the right time to unload it, I suppose, which makes her just as guilty as her husband of felony grand theft. What do you think of her now?" He stood behind the camera. "Okay, let's start filming. Wait for my signal." He looked through the lens, made a couple of adjustments, then pointed his finger at her. "Action!"

Nora lifted the paper, yet it shook so badly that the words blurred together. She finally planted her elbow into her side, hoping to steady it. Then she began reading, *"Hello, Miss Steele, Bella and I are okay, and we're being treated kindly, but as you know, he wants the coin collection. If you don't do exactly as I tell you, he is going to..."* Nora stopped and looked over at him as a tear dropped down her face.

"Keep going," he whispered.

She cleared her throat and swallowed hard. *"He is going to kill us both. You need to put the coins in a paper bag and bring them to Hollenbeck Park at six-thirty tomorrow morning. Walk to the middle of the footbridge and set the bag down, then leave the park. If you do not come alone, if you do not bring the collection in its entirety, or if you bring fake coins...you will never see me or Bella again. Please, Miss Steele, I...don't want to die."*

A PERILOUS PREMIERE

Freddie put his hand into the air. "Okay, three...two...one...cut! Perfect, Nora! That's a wrap. You did very well."

Nora burst into tears and held her head down, cuddling Bella.

Freddie fiddled with the camera and took the reel of film with him over to the table. "You must be hungry. I went out earlier and bought Chinese for us. There's plenty of chop suey, which is my favorite, along with several shrimp egg rolls and a bucket of fried rice. The little dog would probably like some rice. There are even a couple of fortune cookies."

Nora dried her eyes. She couldn't eat a thing, but she knew Bella was hungry. She got up and joined him at the table. After she put some rice on a paper plate, she set it on the floor. Bella gobbled it up as though she hadn't eaten in a month. Nora glanced upstairs. Boris was still howling, and she wanted to take a plate up to him, but she was afraid to ask.

Freddie pulled out a chair and dumped a pile of chop suey on a paper plate. "What's wrong? Sit down and dig in. Far East Café has the best Chinese food in California."

"I...I can't..."

"Don't worry," he laughed. "I didn't poison the food." But he followed her gaze upstairs and threw his chopsticks down. "Damn it!"

Nora turned to him and stiffened. His black eyes held that same vacant look again, the one that had frightened her half to death earlier. He shoved the chair back and stood up.

"I'm going to get my gun and shoot that dirty, rotten dog to shut him up for good."

As he stormed away, Nora rushed after him. "No, Freddie, don't! Please, don't hurt Boris. He'll quiet down soon. I'm sure of it." She cringed as she slipped her arm through his. "I'm really hungry now, Freddie. Let's both sit down, and we'll have a nice dinner together, okay?" And she led him back to the table.

27

A Daring Move

Vivian and Preston sat in the car in front of the steel factory on Shepherd Drive, waiting for Nick to pull up behind them in Barney's car. The sun had set half an hour ago, but the sky glowed a deep shade of orange, lighting the scenery just enough for them to get a good look at the large brick warehouse just beyond the factory.

"The first-floor lights are on," Vivian said. "There's also a dim light in one of the rooms on the second floor."

Preston nodded. "Freddie's pickup truck is parked by the front door."

"As I see it, we have three choices, Preston. We can break into the building through a window or back door and hope Nora doesn't get hurt, but we both know that's too risky, especially since Boris would most likely alert Freddie before we even got inside. Another choice is for you to go to the front door and try to convince Freddie to make a trade using Carl and the coins. I'm sure you see the problem with that. Freddie views you as the enemy. You said yourself that he's trying to beat you at your own game."

"You have quite a memory, don't you?"

"When it matters," she stated.

"I'm almost afraid to ask. What's the third choice?"

Vivian lifted her chin. "Let me talk to him."

Preston nearly jumped out of his seat. "Are you out of your mind? There's no way in hell you're going anywhere near him. He's a lunatic who doesn't have any regard for human life and specifically targets women. It would be like volunteering to stand in front of a firing squad."

"Oh, don't be so dramatic. The fact that I'm a woman is exactly why it might work. He's trying to prove his superiority and right off the bat, he won't view me as a threat, not like he would with you or Nick. He also thinks I have the coins. That's the prize he wants for winning this game. I know I can convince him that I value Nora and Bella over the money." She tapped her chin. "I'll need to come up with some sort of story about how I found out he was here, though."

While Preston ranted and raved about what a bad idea it was, Vivian mulled over a few different ideas and played each one out in her mind. Nick finally pulled up behind them and walked over to find out why Preston was in such an uproar. Then Nick joined in, voicing his own objections.

"The two of you sound like a couple of squawking chickens," she told them. "If you would both be quiet for a minute, I could think this through."

"There is nothing to think about," Preston argued. "You're not going anywhere."

She glanced behind her. "Does Freddie know what kind of car Barney drives?"

Preston opened his mouth to continue arguing with her, but Nick spoke first. "I doubt it. Barney has an office set up in his apartment and rarely goes out into the field anymore."

"Good," she said with a smile. "Although the way you worded that, Nick, it sounds like you all work for some sort of law enforcement agency. Am I right?"

Neither of them replied.

"Well, at least I silenced you both. I'm going to drive to the warehouse in Barney's car, and I want Carl to come with me. I'm hoping you have some rope to tie Carl's feet. I don't want him going anywhere until I'm good and ready." She grabbed her handbag, opened the door, and got out of the car. "All three of you are welcome to follow me over there on foot but stay out of sight and don't make a sound. Once Nora and Bella are safe, you can do whatever you want with Freddie. Unfortunately, I'll probably need to give him the coins, but I'm sure you can retrieve them."

"Vivian, wait!" Preston flew out of the car and went over to her.

She stood firm and faced him. "Before you say another word, Preston, hear me out. Nora's life is on the line. As a matter of fact, it's my fault, not yours, that you're all involved in this. If my rat of a husband hadn't stolen those coins, none of us would be here. It's my responsibility to try to rectify this."

"It's such a bad plan, Vivian."

"I can't think of a better one. Can you?"

Vivian left him there without waiting for his response and determinedly marched over to talk to Barney, who was sitting in the passenger seat of his car. He hesitated and glanced over at Preston before giving her both the keys to the handcuffs and the car keys. She asked him to help Carl into the front seat, and Nick tied his ankles together with a rope he had in his trunk.

Once Vivian was settled in the driver's seat, she turned the car on and moved a couple of feet forward, but she stopped in front of Preston and spoke softly. "If this plan doesn't work, do me a favor. Tell Arthur Romano what happened. He lives on Pearl Street in Santa Monica. I don't want him reading about it in some newspaper. He's been like a father to me." And she drove off.

Vivian rolled up her window and took a dozen deep breaths on the short ride to the warehouse. By now, it was nearly pitch dark out, and she parked right beside Freddie's pickup truck. "Now, just sit here as quiet as a mouse, Carl. I'm going to do my best to make sure no one gets hurt, not even Freddie. If you cooperate, I promise I'll talk the judge into reducing your new sentence by several years. If you don't, you'll spend the rest of your life in prison for murder."

Next, Vivian took two coins out of the velvet pouch and tucked them into her skirt pocket, along with the keys to the handcuffs. She stepped out of the car, holding her gun in one hand and the velvet pouch in the other, and she honked the horn twice.

"Freddie! It's Vivian Steele!"

She walked to the front door and set both the velvet pouch and her gun down on the ground next to the building, out of sight. Then she pounded on the door, repeating her name and yelling to Freddie that she had both the coin collection and his cousin with her, and she wanted to make a trade.

During a moment of silence, Vivian could hear the sound of a dog howling. She knew it was Boris, but it was faint and coming from one of the rooms upstairs.

"What are you doing here?" Freddie called to her from the other side of the door.

"I told you. I have the coins, and I want to make a trade." He didn't say anything, and she knew why. "Nora would never take Bella anywhere without my permission. That's when I realized you were behind all of this, Freddie. I also knew you were staying at the motel on Sunset Boulevard, so I went there and found Carl, your cousin. I explained I wanted to give you the coins in exchange for Nora and Bella, and he told me that you were here. I brought Carl with me."

"Who else is with you?"

"Preston doesn't know anything about this. I came here by myself with Carl. Let me come inside, and we'll talk." She waited there and saw him peek out the window.

He unlocked the door and opened it just a crack, enough for her to see the gun in his hand. Then he looked over at his cousin. "Why is Carl just sitting there?"

"I tied his hands and feet so he wouldn't go anywhere," she told him. "Nora and Bella are extremely important to me, and I wanted to make sure I had enough to give you in exchange for them."

He slowly opened the door wider and held the gun on her as she entered the building. "You better not have any weapons on you."

"I didn't come here to kill you."

"Where are the coins?"

"Where's Nora?" she asked, taking a quick glance around.

He shut the door behind her. "Upstairs, safe and sound, so is your little mutt. How do I know you have the coins? I searched your place and couldn't find them."

"They were hidden behind my wedding photograph."

"I'll shoot you right here if you're lying."

"I'm sure you would." She reached into her pocket and struggled to steady her hand as she held out the two coins. "There are twenty-five coins altogether. The rest are in the vicinity. I'll give them to you when I'm sure Nora and Bella are safe. Then, I'll let your cousin go. I don't care about the coins, Freddie. I've been trying to think of a way to get rid of them without being arrested. My husband stole them, not me. I just want to take Nora and Bella with me and never look back on this again."

Freddie studied the coins. "Wait right here."

Vivian watched him climb up the stairs, knowing full well it couldn't be this easy. Freddie's behavior had been so unpredictable, he was surely devising some sort of scheme right now. Boris started barking wildly upstairs and sounded like a vicious animal. She also heard heavy chains clanking around and wondered if Freddie had chained Boris in one of the rooms.

Those thoughts broke away when Bella came racing down the stairs, whining excitedly all the way. Vivian bent down, and Bella licked her face and hands and jumped on her. She picked Bella up and held her close while watching Freddie escort Nora over to her, holding the barrel of his gun against her chin. It nearly crushed Vivian's stamina, seeing her dear friend looking so tired and scared. If she had her gun with her, she would have put a bullet through Freddie's black heart before he even had a chance to pull the trigger.

As it was, she stood there wondering what sort of trick he had up his sleeve.

Freddie suddenly released Nora and kept the gun on both of them. Nora ran over to her, crying hysterically.

Vivian set Bella down and hugged her. "I'm so sorry, Nora. It'll be all right." She saw Freddie move toward them and pulled Nora behind her to protect her.

"Give me the coins," Freddie ordered.

"They're right outside," Vivian said. "I'm going to open the door and let Nora and Bella go free. You can keep your gun on me while I retrieve the coins if you must, but I'll stay close to the doorway so you can see me." She waited for his consent since she didn't want to upset him when they were so close to ending this.

He stepped forward and motioned for her to go to the door. "I'm right behind you."

"I know. Relax. I'll give them to you." Vivian was almost in tears herself, as she slowly opened the door and told Nora to go outside, and Bella went with her. "I'm just going to put one foot out the door, Freddie."

As soon as she did, she noticed Nick standing in the dark shadows along the building. He caught Nora in his arms and whisked her away. With that, Vivian breathed again. She bent down, picked up the velvet pouch, and eyed her pistol.

"Hurry up!" Freddie said, standing right behind her.

"I've got it."

Just as she reached for her gun, Freddie grabbed a handful of her hair, yanked her back inside, and shoved her to the floor. Then he slammed the door shut and locked it.

"What are you doing?" she yelled. "We had a deal!"

He laughed as he snatched the pouch from her and looked inside. "I don't make deals with big-shot dames like you."

"I still have your cousin handcuffed in my car."

"The hell with him. I've got what I want right here." He stuck the pouch into his pocket and pointed the gun at her. "I might even make sure this whole thing gets pinned on him, and I'll keep the coins for myself..."

While Freddie rambled on about how clever he was, Vivian saw movement out of the corner of her eye and noticed Boris slinking down the steps and stealthily walking toward Freddie like a tiger stalking its prey. She slid backward across the floor a couple of feet to get out of the way, and Freddie laughed at her, thinking she was trying to escape.

Then he cocked his gun, and Vivian prayed Boris would make his move before he pulled the trigger.

A split second later, Boris snarled, catching Freddie's attention. He spun around in a panic and pointed his gun at Boris, but it was too late. Boris leaped into the air, jumped on Freddie, knocked him to the ground, and clamped his teeth around his arm, growling and digging his sharp teeth deep into his flesh.

Freddie shouted and screamed bloody murder and dropped his gun to fight against Boris.

Vivian scurried over to get his gun. At the same time, Preston ran into the room from the back of the warehouse and rushed over to them.

"That's enough, Boris!" Preston told him.

Boris backed away yet didn't take his eyes off Freddie, who was lying there, bleeding and trying to catch his breath.

Vivian got down on one knee and hugged Boris. "Good boy."

"Are you okay, Vivian?" Preston asked.

"I am now, thanks to Boris."

"It looks like he broke away from the chains around his neck just in time to come to your rescue. He's quite a hero." Preston grinned at her. "That was a pretty good plan."

"You could have stepped in a few seconds sooner."

He laughed. "I had a heck of a time trying to kick open the back door."

28

Until We Meet Again...

Monday, May 9

Vivian walked around the display room at her boutique with a renewed sense of pride and contentment. It had been such a long time since she felt this happy.

Over the weekend, so many friends had come to help her and Nora clean up every inch of the boutique and her apartment, including Carole and Clark, Preston, Nick, Barney, Maria from next door, Henry from the shoe store, and Nancy, who was now working as a salesclerk for her. They all had such a great time, too, and everything looked even better than before.

Freddie had confessed to killing Tilly Trimble and Priscilla Peachtree, and both he and his cousin were going to be locked away in jail for who knows how many years. Even though she'd promised to talk to the judge on Carl's behalf for cooperating with her, she changed her mind and decided not to keep that promise after all the harm they'd done.

She also put Rocco Rizzoli out of her mind, and the fact that he'd tricked her into thinking she had a department store contract in her pocket. It wasn't worth dwelling over. But she imagined Rocco would deliberately run into her again at some point, and she was going to make sure he regretted it.

"Vivian!" Nora called to her from the back room. "Come have some coffee and a bagel with Nancy and me before we open."

"Coming!" Vivian joined them and poured herself a cup of coffee. She sat down and started petting Bella sitting on the floor beside them. "I can't believe how wonderful everything looks." She smiled and placed her hand on Nora's. "I'm especially grateful to the two of you for all your help. Preston and Nick will be here around nine-thirty to pick me up. The jury is going to announce their decision in the Harry Raymond case, and we want to hear the verdict. Hopefully, they find Captain Kynette guilty."

"Nancy and I will handle everything while you're gone," Nora told her. The bell on the front door jingled, and she got up. "We don't open for another ten minutes, but our customers are probably anxious to shop here again. Come on, Nancy. Here's your first customer."

The two of them disappeared into the other room while Vivian sipped her coffee and glanced around the back room, so grateful that everything was back to normal.

Nora stood in the doorway. "There's an older gentleman here to see you, Vivian."

She wondered who it was and walked over to Nora. She saw the man wandering around the display room and caught her breath. "Oh, my..."

"Who is he?" Nora asked.

"The real Glen Rutherford from Bullock's. I wonder what he's doing here." She straightened her skirt and approached him. "Good morning, Mister Rutherford. How...how nice to see you again."

He smiled at her. "The pleasure is all mine, Miss Steele. You have a lovely shop here. After you left my office the other day, I kept thinking about what you said, and how someone had tricked you by impersonating me. I felt terrible for you, so I had my assistant find out where you lived, and here I am. I didn't realize you owned a fashion boutique."

"You're very kind, but you shouldn't have gone to so much trouble. I've put the whole thing out of my mind."

"As you should, but may I ask? Are you a designer, or do you order your merchandise from other stores?"

"These are all my custom designs."

"Really..." He walked around the entire room, stopping in each section and pulling a few dresses and outfits off the rack. "This is amazing. I'm surprised I haven't heard about your shop before. John Bullock is going to want to speak with you. I assume you have a portfolio."

"I can have one ready by the end of the day."

"Splendid! Here is my business card. Call me later, and I'll set up a meeting. You are an extremely talented young woman."

Vivian thanked him and walked him to the front door. Then she spun around and clapped her hands with excitement, thrilled to her toes. She hurried into the back room to tell Nora and Nancy. They were as excited as she was, and they offered to help her make a new portfolio when she returned.

At nine-thirty, Vivian saw Nick pull up out front with Preston. She got into the car and sat between them in the front seat. "Okay, I've been dying to know," she said as they drove to the city. "Who ended up with Boris?"

"Nick and I flipped a coin," Preston told her.

"Who won?"

Nick chuckled. "I did."

"That's wonderful. Boris is living with you now?"

Preston grumbled under his breath. "No...the loser took him. Me! Of course, my mother is thrilled."

Vivian burst out laughing. "You said Boris was a hero. You should be honored to have him with you."

"Do you have any idea how much that big lug eats?"

"Stop griping, Preston," Nick laughed. "You can afford it."

They reached the courthouse, and Nick parked the car down the side street. They walked up the front steps to the main entrance and went inside. There was a small crowd of people waiting for the security guard to open the courtroom. Vivian looked around. She wasn't in the mood to deal with the mayor or his brother, but she assumed they would want to hear the verdict. Instead, she spotted Lucky in the crowd. He saw her, too, and motioned to her.

"I'll be right back."

"Where are you going?" Preston asked.

Vivian ignored him and made her way over to Lucky. "I'm surprised to see you here. Is everything all right?"

"Yeah, everything's fine. When I heard the news, I knew you'd be here this morning. It's quite a turn of events, isn't it?"

She was confused. "What are you talking about?"

"The new charges against Kynette. Didn't you know? After the jury announces their verdict in the Harry Raymond case, they're indicting Captain Kynette for two other murders. Over the weekend, some *unnamed investigator* came across new evidence proving Captain Kynette shot and killed both your husband and the drugstore owner. I can't believe you didn't hear about it. Surprised the heck out of me."

Vivian looked over at Preston and Nick. "An unnamed investigator, huh?"

"I guess it's pretty solid evidence, too, from what I heard."

"That's wonderful. Lucky, thank you so much for everything."

"Call if you need me, Blondie."

"I will. Take care of yourself." By the time Vivian joined Preston and Nick again, she was surprised to see Carole with them. "What are you doing here, Carole?"

"Preston called me and told me about the indictment against Captain Kynette for George's murder. I wanted to be here for you, Viv."

She glanced up at Preston. "Why didn't you tell me?"

"I wanted to surprise you."

"It's certainly a surprise, but I feel bad about Elliott Kimball now."

"Don't..." Preston stated. "He died because he resisted arrest and killed an officer. If he'd been patient, he would have walked away from the charges."

"Besides, he was a scumbag," Nick added.

The security guard finally opened the courtroom door. The four of them followed along with the crowd and found seats close to the front of the room. For a while, Vivian kept her sights on Captain Kynette, sitting at the counsel table with his lawyer. Once the jurors were seated, and the judge took his place at his bench, he asked for the verdict.

A gentleman in the jury box stood up and read it out loud. "We, the jurors, find Captain Earl Kynette guilty on the charge of attempted murder. We find him guilty on the charge of accessory to commit murder, and we find him guilty on the charge of malicious use of explosives. Guilty on all three counts, Your Honor."

Everyone in the crowd stood up and cheered, and the judge pounded his hammer several times to quiet the courtroom. After the jurors were excused, the prosecutor stood up to speak with the judge about additional murder charges against the defendant. Vivian listened closely, and the moment George's name was mentioned, Captain Kynette turned his glare on her.

She smiled back at him.

Everyone left the courtroom, and the four of them made their way outside. Carole offered to take Vivian back to her apartment, but they reached Nick's car first, and Vivian slowed her pace. "I'll catch up to you, Carole. I just need a moment with these two clowns."

"See you later, Carole!" Nick called out as he got into his car.

Vivian faced Preston. "I'm grateful to you for making sure George's involvement wasn't publicized. More than anything, I didn't want his daughter to find out what he'd done."

"Since he paid the highest price for his mistakes, it wasn't necessary. I can't thank you enough for helping us catch Freddie and retrieve the coins. The attorney was happy to get them back before the deadline."

"Come on, Preston. I've got to know. Who are you really working for?"

"I already told you. My father was a good friend of Chester Willoughby. I did it as a favor to him. Why don't you tell me who you really are?"

She shrugged her shoulders innocently. "I'm a fashion designer."

Preston flashed her a dashing smile. "You know Boris is going to want to visit Bella sometime. So, until we meet again…"

Vivian reached up and straightened his tie. "Don't call me, Preston. I'll call you." She left his side and walked by the car. "It was wonderful meeting you, Nick!"

He threw his hand in the air. "Likewise, Vivian!"

THE END

A Special Note to Readers

Thank you very much for reading *A Perilous Premiere*. I hope you enjoyed it. When I decided to begin writing a new mystery series, I wanted to make sure it was very different from the Jax Diamond Mysteries, my current series, with fresh and unique characters and plots. I quickly realized that I'd become so attached to Jax and his crew, it took me a while to embrace the new characters, but long before I finished, I fell in love with them. I hope you did, too.

If you're familiar with my other books, you know I try to include as many historical facts as I can in the stories, and I always share some interesting tidbits along with some tunes or short videos from the era.

Despite the tough economic times during the Depression, it's estimated that up to eighty million Americans went to the movies every week. There were so many wonderful actors and actresses back in the 1930s and 1940s, and I have several favorites. For me, Carole Lombard has always stood out above all others, and I had to include her as a character in the book. She was not only beautiful, talented, fun-loving (nicknamed a 'screwball'), honest, foul-mouthed, and married to Clark Gable, she endured a few tragedies in her life, and the last one ended her life.

Carole began acting at the young age of twelve and starred in several films throughout the 1920s. In 1927, Carole was a passenger in a serious car accident. The windshield shattered and shards of glass cut Carole's face from her nose and across her left cheek to her eye. After plastic surgery and a long recovery, she was able to return to her acting career. Still, she needed to apply plenty of makeup to cover the scar.

Carole married William Powell, from the famous *Thin Man* series, in 1931. Their marriage ended in divorce in 1933, but they always remained close friends.

In 1934, Carole's fiancée, Russ Columbo, an American baritone, songwriter, violinist, and actor, was shot under 'peculiar circumstances' by a longtime friend, photographer Lansing Brown Jr., shortly before Russ was picking Carole up for dinner. Here is the song he wrote for Carole before

A PERILOUS PREMIERE

he died, *Too Beautiful for Words* https://www.youtube.com/watch?v=NRwWE7A24AQ

Carole and Clark Gable only made one movie together in 1932, *No Man of Her Own*, and apparently, they didn't get along very well. Yet, they met up again in 1936 and became inseparable. It was said that Clark thrived being around Carole's youthful, charming, and frank personality. He once stated: "*You can trust that little screwball with your life or your hopes or your weaknesses, and she wouldn't even think about letting you down.*"

In 1939, Clark proposed to Carole in Booth Fifty-Four at the popular Brown Derby restaurant, and they were married six weeks later. They bought a twenty-acre ranch in Encino, California, and adopted several barnyard animals. Almost immediately, Carole wanted to start a family, but her attempts failed, and she discovered she was unable to have children. Here is a clip of their history together: https://www.youtube.com/watch?v=drmzbxhxyZM&t=14s

When the U.S. entered World War II, Carole traveled to her home state of Indiana for a war bond rally with her mother and Clark Gable's press agent, Otto Winkler. On January 16, 1942, Carole decided to fly home early to see Clark. Her mother, an astrologist, begged her not to go on flight number three because it was an unlucky number. She refused to listen to her mother's warning and insisted they board the flight.

Shortly after takeoff, the plane crashed in Las Vegas. Tragically, everyone on board, including the three of them, were killed. Carole was only thirty-three years old at the time. Clark Gable was devastated by her death and never married again. President Roosevelt awarded Carole the Medal Of Freedom for being the first woman killed in the line of duty during the war.

She was an incredible woman, inside and out, and I've always admired her so much. As for Clark Gable, my favorite actor, he was wonderful in *Gone with the Wind*, but my all-time favorite movie of his was, *It Happened One Night* with Claudette Colbert. Here is a clip from that movie (love it!):

https://www.youtube.com/watch?v=Wcrth90C3D4

On a political note: Many of my references were true. Frank Shaw was elected mayor in 1933 and appointed his brother, Joe, as secretary and chief of staff. He also reappointed James Davis, who was "nationally notorious" for police corruption, as police chief of the LAPD. Skipping over their long list of crimes, in 1937, it all came to a head after Harry Raymond, a former police officer investigating corruption on the force, was the victim of a car bomb and seriously injured. LAPD Captain Earl Kynette was indeed found guilty on the charges in 1938 and served sixteen years in prison.

It took several more months before Frank Shaw became the first mayor of a major city to be removed from office, thanks to Clifford Clinton and the CIVIC group's efforts to gather enough evidence to bring to the grand jury. As for Clifton's Brookdale Cafeteria, it remained the largest cafeteria in the world until 2018 when they finally closed their doors.

Lastly, here are two popular 1930s tunes that were mentioned in the book. Nora Griswald's favorite, Kenny Baker singing *Love Walked In* (it's a hoot): **https://www.youtube.com/watch?v=7W-kbu12-cU**

And Fred Astaire and Ginger Rogers in the movie *Top Hat*, singing *Cheek to Cheek*: **https://www.youtube.com/watch?v=LDIlkTqjldQ**

Vivian and Preston will be back in *A BLOODY BANQUET, Book Two* (release date to be announced soon). And if you've enjoyed the Jax Diamond Mysteries series, *WILDCARD, Book 8* will be released in April 2025 (possibly sooner). Don't miss Jax and Laura's eventful honeymoon! Pre-order at Amazon: WILDCARD

https://www.amazon.com/WILDCARD-JAX-DIAMOND-MYSTERIES-Book-ebook/dp/B0DDHJKV3T

In closing, thank you again for taking the time to read the book. I hope you have a safe and happy holiday!

All my best,

Gail

Milton Keynes UK
Ingram Content Group UK Ltd.
UKHW021849231124
451423UK00001B/299